FOR THE LOVE
OF
LLAMAS

By Patti Jo Moore

Published by Forget Me Not Romances, a division of Winged Publications

Copyright © 2020 by Patti Jo Moore

All rights reserved. No part of this publication may be resold, reproduced, stored in a retrieval system, or transmitted in any form or by any means, electronic, mechanical, recording, or otherwise, without the prior written permission of the author. Piracy is illegal. Thank you for respecting the hard work of this author.

This is a work of fiction. All characters, names, dialogue, incidents, and places either are the product of the author's imagination or are used fictitiously. Any resemblance to actual events, locales, or people, living or dead, is entirely coincidental.

ISBN: 979-8-8690-7320-4

This book is dedicated to my precious granddaughter, Eleanor, whose fascination with llamas inspired my own. You are such a sweet blessing and true miracle, Eleanor. Pippi loves you so much!

I'm forever grateful to my Lord and Savior, Jesus Christ. You've created such a wonderful world, filled with special blessings like grandbabies, cats, and llamas!

Chapter One

When Claire Durham opened her eyes on Monday morning, the last thing she expected that day was learning she'd inherited a farm. As she did on each workday, Claire groggily climbed out of bed to get dressed for her job. Her mundane, nothing-spectacular job. Still, she was thankful to have one. Grabbing her travel mug of coffee, she exited her small apartment and headed to work.

Making the ten-minute drive into the business district of upscale Fernwood, Georgia, Claire released a sigh. She tried to count her blessings, but lately she'd been wondering if there'd be any new ones in her future. Well, at least she'd not had any annoying phone calls from her ex-boyfriend in the past month.

Hopefully Kyle had finally gotten the message that they were finished. She was better off unattached than in a relationship with someone who tried to control her. A shiver ran through her despite the warm September sunshine coming through her car window. A controlling male was the last thing she needed in her life.

When she entered the small building that housed Manny Logistics, the aroma of freshly-brewed coffee greeted her. But there was something else. Something sweet and floral. A fragrance that reminded her of a florist shop.

As she signed in at the counter, Claire realized why she'd smelled flowers. Vases and baskets of colorful blooms surrounded Gretchen, the receptionist. Had someone died? Claire's heart raced.

Surely not. Gretchen was giggling and chattering to another employee, who gushed while admiring the roses, carnations, and various other lovely blooms on the counter. Wowzers! What was going on? Gretchen noticed Claire and beamed. "Good morning, Claire."

"Good morning, Gretchen. Um…is today your birthday?" Oh my, those coral-colored roses were absolutely gorgeous. Claire returned her focus to the receptionist.

The thirty-something woman covered her mouth with a manicured hand and giggled again. "No, even better. Hank and I learned yesterday that we're going to have a baby! Needless to say, all of our relatives are thrilled about this news." Apparently so. And likely one of the relatives owned a flower shop.

"Congratulations!" Claire smiled at Gretchen, genuinely happy for her.

"Thanks, honey. I'm a little overwhelmed with all

these flowers, but our families had given up on any babies, since I'm pushing forty." Her southern accent seemed more pronounced in her excitement, and her hand gestures accompanied her words.

Another employee stepped up to offer congratulations, so Claire headed to her small office to put away her handbag, then grab some coffee from the breakroom. Even as she prepared her coffee, her mind returned to Gretchen's news. How special that would be—learning you were expecting your first baby. Would Claire ever know that feeling?

At the age of twenty-nine, her prospects were becoming scarce. Since her last boyfriend had ended up being a jerk, Claire had relief rather than a broken heart. He'd been deceitful and controlling, dating Claire along with other women, while telling her she was the only one. When she'd become aware of how much he enjoyed alcohol and saw its effects on his personality, it was time to end the relationship. She'd not had a minute of regret.

"Hey Claire, you want to join me for lunch today? I'm hungry for pizza, so let's head to Skip's at eleven-thirty."

Claire glanced up to see her best friend and co-worker Marcy Webster in her doorway. "Hey Marcy. I thought you only ate out on Fridays. What gives?"

Marcy shrugged. "Yeah, I'm saving the sandwich I brought for tomorrow. It'll keep in the breakroom refrigerator. I just had a craving for pizza." A sheepish grin followed her words.

"Okay, I'll join you. I brought a salad, but I'll eat it tomorrow."

"Maybe we'll beat the lunch crowd." Marcy took a swig of the canned cola she held.

"Sounds good. I'll be ready." Claire turned to her computer, ready to tackle that day's assignments. She'd been a bit restless lately, so maybe going out for lunch would help her stay focused later in the day.

A few hours later, the two women enjoyed pizza at the small eatery near their office. Marcy eyed Claire after finishing her first slice of pepperoni pizza. "Are you okay? You look like you're deep in thought."

Claire nodded. "For some reason I've been feeling restless lately. I'm thankful to have a job and an apartment, but I keep wondering if there's more I'm supposed to do with my life." She shook her head and forced a chuckle. "I've even wondered if I should go on a mission trip."

Marcy appeared thoughtful. "That might be interesting. But you already do a lot to help others. Look at the volunteer work you did last year at the nursing home, and all the Saturdays you've volunteered to tutor children with reading. I haven't done half the good deeds you've done. Not to mention, your two cats are rescues, so you've even saved animal lives." She bit into another slice of pizza.

Claire grinned at the thought of the two lovable felines who shared her small apartment. "I like helping others, because I feel I'm doing something useful.

Besides, I don't have relatives in the area as you do, so that gives me more free time." She blew out a sigh. "I always figured by the time I reached this age, I'd be married and have a child or two." She regretted speaking that thought aloud, knowing Marcy might try to play matchmaker. *Again.*

Marcy rolled her eyes. "Yeah, sorry those two guys I introduced you to didn't work out."

Claire reached over and patted her friend's arm. "It's okay. I appreciate that you made the effort to introduce me to guys you knew. It's not your fault they didn't work out." She suppressed a shudder at the memory of both men—one a total introvert, and the other obsessed with race cars. Not that those were negative qualities, but there was no compatibility with either of them.

Changing the subject, Claire mentioned the approaching holidays. "I know it's still September, but Thanksgiving and Christmas will be here before we know it."

Being an avid food-lover, Marcy chattered about holiday recipes she planned to prepare, her face lighting up at the mention of several desserts.

Ten minutes later the women headed back to the office. As they walked the short distance toward the logistics building, a sleek sports coupe passed them. Claire caught a glimpse of the driver, a dark-haired man who didn't look familiar to her. What really caught her attention was his car tag. DEX3. *I wonder what it stands for? Maybe his initials?* Yet no one she knew had a last name that began with an X. *How unusual.*

Arriving at their building, the women returned to their separate offices. Claire stifled a yawn and hoped the pizza wouldn't make her sleepy, but it had been a nice break leaving the office. She needn't have worried about drowsiness, though, because the phone call she received minutes later jolted her wide awake.

~ ~ ~

"A farm? Are you sure?" Claire's hand shook as she listened to an attorney. The pizza she'd eaten thirty minutes earlier sat like a lead weight in her middle and she only caught certain words. Distant relative. Inheritance. Farmland. Could this be some kind of scam? She'd heard news reports of scammers using various tactics to trick people over the phone.

"Yes, Miss Durham, that is correct. Mr. Lloyd Boatwright's will clearly states that his property—including the land and everything on it—is to go to his half-sister's offspring. According to the information we have, that would be you."

This was too much to absorb. Claire knew her late mother had a half-brother, but Claire had never met the man—at least not that she could recall. Maybe as an infant she'd been around him, but she had no recollection of the man. None. She gripped the phone and her heart pounded as she tried to think of a coherent response.

"I-I'm stunned." Clearly an understatement, but that

was the best she could do at the moment.

His all-business voice changed to a more compassionate tone. "I'm sure this is a shock, Miss Durham, but I wanted to notify you right away. Would you be able to meet with me in person? There are papers you'll need to sign, and then—if you'd like—I will provide more information regarding your inheritance."

"That would be good." After jotting down directions to his law office, in addition to the time of their meeting, Claire thanked him for calling, then clicked off her cell phone.

For a few minutes, she sat and stared at her blank computer screen. A jumble of thoughts bounced inside her head. Disbelief, shock, and amazement. Maybe she was dreaming, and she'd awaken soon.

"Claire? Are you okay?" Marcy appeared in her doorway, frowning as she clutched a canned cola. "I got a drink from the machine and saw you just sitting there. Did the pizza make you sick? Do you need a drink?" Her friend stepped into the small office, thrusting the unopened can toward Claire.

At least that offered a bit of humor, and Claire gave her a shaky smile. "No, thanks. You enjoy your cola. I-I just had the strangest phone call." After gesturing for Marcy to close the door, Claire proceeded to tell her about the attorney's message.

Marcy's eyes widened. "Wow. Just wow. You've inherited land, Claire. You could be rich!"

Claire shook her head. "I have no idea what the land

looks like, or what it's worth, so I don't think that's the case."

Marcy sobered and ducked her head. "I'm sorry. I didn't even offer condolences for your uncle's passing."

"It's okay. To be honest, I didn't even know him. He was my mother's half-brother, and they weren't close." A twinge of sadness poked her at the mention of her mother. She'd been gone for eight years, but Claire still missed her.

As though sensing Claire's thoughts, Marcy reached out and patted her shoulder. Then after a few seconds of silence, she added, "Well, I'm glad the pizza we ate didn't make you sick, because I'd feel bad since it was my idea."

Claire managed a genuine smile. "No, I enjoyed the pizza. Thanks for stopping in to check on me, and if you would, please don't share what I just told you."

Marcy pretended to zip her lips. "Are you sure you don't need a canned drink?"

"No, but I might get some coffee." She rose from her chair and headed to the breakroom when Marcy returned to her own office. Claire was relieved no one else was in the hallway, because she didn't want anyone besides Marcy to know what she'd just learned. Her other co-workers meant well, but some of them could be gossipy, and Claire didn't need word of her inheritance flying around the building.

After fixing herself a cup of coffee, she returned to her computer, needing to complete some assignments and wanting to stay focused. But as she entered numbers and other data, she had to stop a few times to make corrections. Her mind was obviously not on her work at the moment. How could it be? She'd learned that she was now a landowner.

Who knew she'd receive a call from an attorney that afternoon—a call informing her that she'd inherited land from a relative she didn't know? It wasn't only a piece of land, but a farm. What on earth would Claire Durham do with a farm?

~ ~ ~

Chapter 2

Carlton Poindexter Jennings, III focused on the papers spread across his polished mahogany desk. Although he used his computer quite often, sometimes he preferred the old-school method of actual papers containing the information he needed to see. But today, that information wasn't to his liking. He must do better.

He released a sigh and ran a hand down his clean-shaven face. Deep in thought, he didn't see his secretary at the door until she spoke.

"Excuse me, Dexter. Would you like anything from the sandwich shop downstairs?" The fifty-something woman was not only a hard-working employee, but she was thoughtful and didn't mind running errands for him now and then. He'd insisted she call him the name he went by, rather than Mr. Jennings. Dexter had enough formalities in his life without his secretary being formal, too.

He smiled at the plainly-dressed woman. "No, thank you, Dora. But I appreciate your asking. I'm actually headed to meet my father for lunch at the country club, but should return by two-thirty."

Dora returned a smiling nod, then hurried to the elevator of the upscale building. Her footsteps echoed softly on the polished floor. Maybe it was just as well she didn't dress more formally, as some of the women did, because their stiletto heels created a loud echo whenever they walked.

Rubbing his temples, Dexter knew a headache was brewing. Maybe after eating lunch at the club it would subside. Grabbing the papers from his desk, he placed them inside a folder which went into a drawer. He wasn't accomplishing anything by staring at his recent listings and sales, so he may as well head to the club to meet his father.

Hopefully, Carlton Poindexter Jennings, II, or Carl, as he was called, would be in a good mood today. It seemed that the older his father became, the more he expected of his only son. Not that Dexter was a slacker, by any means. No, he was driven—sometimes too much so. But when he'd celebrated his twenty-ninth birthday this past January, he'd had somewhat of an epiphany, realizing he was no longer the young kid but approaching thirty.

As though emphasizing his current thoughts, his cell phone rang, showing Howard's name on the caller ID. Dexter had pulled into his usual parking space at the country club, cut his engine off, and grabbed his phone. "Hey, Howard. What's up?"

Howard Evans had been Dexter's best friend since

college, when they'd been roommates and fraternity brothers. There had been other friends but none as loyal as Howard. Although Howard's family didn't possess the wealth that Dexter's family had, the men had hit if off and remained close friends after college. Now Howard had a promising career with a computer software developer and lived in an apartment not far from Dexter's. Howard often lamented his single status as his thirtieth birthday approached.

"Hey dude. Just checking to see if we're still on for pizza and watching the game this Saturday."

Dexter chuckled. "Yep, sounds good to me." The men discussed which college team they thought would win. "See you at my place on Saturday." Dexter clicked off his phone, then headed through the elaborate wooden doors of the Fernwood Country Club.

"There's my son." Carl Jennings was chatting with a friend in the lobby and gestured to his son. "Dexter, you know Randolph Waters." The heavy-set, middle-aged man shook Dexter's hand, then joked about trying to line up a golf game with Dexter's father.

After a few more good-natured comments, Mr. Waters exited the club doors, and Dexter and his father headed to a table in the dining room. As usual, a hostess greeted them by name, the young woman's gaze lingering on Dexter.

Although she was likely college-aged, the woman appeared to be a teen-ager in Dexter's eyes. Sure, he'd like a romantic relationship again, but the woman was too young. A fleeting memory of Monique, his most recent girlfriend, flashed through his mind, and he quickly shoved away the less-than-pleasant thoughts. What a gold digger she'd turned out to be, so he was more than a little relieved to be finished with that relationship.

"Glad you could meet for lunch, son. I need to discuss a few business ideas with you, and I find it more enjoyable over a hearty meal." Carl's eyes seemed to light up as he perused the menu. Dexter was surprised his father didn't have the entire menu memorized, considering how often he frequented the club.

After placing their orders with a young man, Dexter sipped his water while his father presented his real estate ideas. "Just because I'm nearing retirement doesn't mean I need to stop making money." Carl gave a jovial snort. Dexter didn't comment that he had no doubt his father would continue making money indefinitely, as would he. That driven business-sense had been drilled into him by his father for many years.

Carl's first idea was a casual thought, involving minimal risk by purchasing a plot of land located south of Atlanta. But his second idea nearly caused Dexter to choke on a sip of water.

"A subdivision? Are you serious about this?" Dexter wasn't sure he'd heard his father correctly.

"That's right, son. Randolph Waters had mentioned it to me a few days ago, and we'd discussed it again before you arrived today. He knows of some available farmland in the small town of Peach Grove and thought it would be prime property to build a subdivision. Word is that the entire area should be booming within the next five years, as more people want to leave the hustle and bustle of big cities and traffic."

"Did Mr. Waters want to join forces on this?" The server was coming with their meals, but he wasn't sure he had much of an appetite now.

"Oh, no. Randolph has enough projects going on at the moment, but he was driving back from visiting a relative in middle Georgia and passed the property. He stopped after noticing a for sale sign and wrote down the information in case I was interested. Since I've not been to that area, I thought maybe you could drive out there and take a look. See what you think."

"What was the name of that town?" Dexter hated to seem skeptical, but this sounded like a huge project out in the middle of nowhere. Just how profitable could it be? He didn't mind working hard, but he expected his efforts to pay off. In a major way and not years down the road.

"Peach Grove. Randolph said the city planning experts believe that particular area will take off in the next few years. So why not get a head start and have a prime development there?" Carl smiled proudly before taking a bite of his Philly-cheese steak sandwich.

"Sounds like a major undertaking, Dad." Dexter had learned in recent years to choose his wording carefully where his father's suggestions were concerned. If he sounded too enthusiastic, his father would expect him to charge headlong into a big project before knowing all the facts.

Carl dabbed his mouth with a linen napkin and nodded. "Yes, it would be, son. But what a golden opportunity this would be. You could still continue your realtor duties with listings and clients, but with a subdivision on the side, no telling how much money you'd be making. Likely enough to take an early retirement."

Making money. That's what it always boiled down to whenever Dexter and his father talked business, which was their usual topic of conversation. Rarely had they chatted about sports or current affairs, but rather investments and profits. Preferably, large profits.

After a few moments of silence as the men continued eating, Dexter felt he should say something. He knew he sounded half-hearted, but he'd never been good at disguising his true feelings with his parents.

"I suppose it wouldn't hurt for me to take a look at this property. Maybe Calvin could go with me, and we could snap some photos and make notes." Calvin was a new employee—Dora's nephew—and shared many of Dora's traits. At least the young man wouldn't chatter non-stop when they went.

His reply obviously pleased his father, who now beamed as he finished his last bite of sandwich. Lifting his water glass in a toast, Carl nodded and said, "Here's to a great idea. I know if there's any chance of this working out, you'll be successful, Dexter. And tell Calvin to take plenty of photos."

Dexter didn't join his father in the 'toast' but instead finished his meal and the last few sips of water. "I'll look into this on Monday, because today I need to wrap up some other business with two clients."

His reply seemed to satisfy his father, who was still smiling. But when Dexter was driving back to the real estate office twenty minutes later, his mind whirled. In a way, the thought of developing a subdivision appealed to him and seemed like an exciting challenge, one that could pay off in major finances. But another thought hovered in the back of his mind.

How would Dexter ever have time for anything else in life—particularly a relationship—if his waking hours were consumed with business? Sure, he was still young and energetic, but he didn't have any extra hours in his days. If his father's idea became a reality, then Dexter would likely be spending time driving back and forth to the property each week. After all, he'd have to check on progress and make sure things were going according to plan. And he just wasn't sure how he felt about that. Shouldn't there be more to life than making money?

~ ~ ~

Claire had been certain she'd be a nervous wreck when meeting with the attorney. But instead, she was a bit dazed. Was this actually happening? Had she really inherited acreage in a small, country town?

But it was, in fact, very real. After locating the attorney's office, she pasted on a smile and entered. An older receptionist greeted her, offering her water or coffee. Claire appreciated the gesture, but politely declined. She'd likely pour the liquid on her clothes if she attempted to drink something.

She only had to wait a few minutes before the attorney, Mr. Chadwick, greeted her and led her down a hallway into his private office. The older man appeared organized, as everything in the small room was immaculate. No scattered papers, and even the attorney himself was impeccably dressed, every hair on his graying head in place. After clearing his throat, he began going over the details of the will.

Claire tried to focus completely and allow the information to sink in, but she was certain her eyes held a glazed look. She was appreciative when Mr. Chadwick paused, giving her time to digest his words. He also frequently asked if she had any questions so far. Of course, she wasn't about to admit that she was still in shock about this entire matter.

"My secretary will also be assisting you, Miss Durham, so in the coming days and weeks, if you have questions, please don't hesitate to phone my office. If I'm not available, Mrs. Barnes is happy to help."

Less than an hour later, Claire exited the office, clasping the folder of papers she'd been given, her mind whirling faster than the autumn breeze around her. She glanced up and realized the sky had clouded over while she'd been in the attorney's office, and from all indications a storm was brewing.

She nervously glanced around the parking lot of the legal building, noting all the cars appeared empty. *Whew.* Would she ever get past the fear that sometimes still threatened to wash over her? The stalking incidents had been years ago—seven, to be exact.

Pray. Deep breaths. She reminded herself what she was supposed to do, but still felt relief when she reached her car and climbed inside. The fact that the sky had darkened while she'd been inside the attorney's office had only made the empty parking lot appear ominous. But she was safe, so she allowed her thoughts to return to her meeting with Mr. Chadwick.

I'm a landowner. I own a small farm. The words danced through her head. What on earth was she going to do? Continue living in her apartment and working at her same job?

Approaching her apartment complex, she uttered softly. "Lord, I've been praying for a change in my life. Is this land somehow connected to the change I need to make?" Although at the moment, she couldn't fathom how this inheritance would provide a different direction in her life. After all, Claire was no farmer.

She would need to keep praying and then clearly think about her options. If she left her current job and apartment and moved to her land, what would she do? How would she support herself? Too many questions.

Besides, she hadn't even seen the land yet.

~ ~ ~

The next day at work, Claire suppressed a giggle at Marcy's expression.

"A farm? Are you serious?" Marcy eyed her in disbelief and shook her head, sending her short, dark hair bouncing around her face. "This is unreal."

She patiently waited to hear more of Marcy's thoughts on the inheritance. Not that Claire wanted or expected anyone else to advise her what to do. That decision must be made by her. And only after much prayer.

Marcy grabbed her bottled water and took a swig, then gave Claire her full attention. "Okay, so what are your thoughts about this land? Have you even seen it? No, of course you haven't, since you just learned about it yesterday. But do you know how large the property is?"

Before Marcy could shoot out more questions, Claire shook her head. "No, I've not seen it, but Mr. Chadwick—the attorney—said it's ten acres. As far as my thoughts, I'm still stunned." She plopped into a nearby chair, thankful no one else had entered the breakroom.

Marcy's eyes widened again. "Ten acres? Wow, Claire. That's a sizable piece of land." Marcy eyed the vending machine but remained in her seat.

"Yeah, I know. I'm trying to get a perspective on it, because I know my Aunt Molly lives on five acres, so this would be twice as big as her property. I'm eager to drive there and look. Very soon."

"If you need someone to accompany you, I'll be glad to ride along." Marcy took another sip of her water, then eyed the vending machine again.

"Funny you should mention that, because I was going to ask if you'd like to join me. I'd love to drive there this Saturday. I don't need to take anymore time off from work, so I'm waiting until the weekend to go. Although I have to admit I can't wait to have a look at the land."

"Just let me know what time you want to leave, and I'll be ready." Marcy smiled before stepping to the machine and depositing coins in the slot. "Want anything? There's a candy bar in this machine calling my name." She giggled.

Claire thanked her but declined. She'd have a difficult time staying focused on her work until Saturday, because she was more than a little curious. She also didn't want to get her hopes up ahead of time because that could lead to disappointment. If she visualized a lovely piece of farmland, and then it turned out to resemble a large patch of weeds, that wouldn't be good.

Still, the fact she'd inherited *anything* was amazing, even though it made her sad that she'd never known the distant relative who'd owned the land. She needed to do some family research, and also see what she could find out about the small town of Peach Grove.

A tiny spark of excitement ran through her. Maybe this was, in fact, the adventure of sorts she'd been wanting. Time would tell, and Saturday couldn't come quickly enough.

~ ~ ~

On Friday morning, Dexter decided to go ahead and drive to Peach Grove and look at the property his father had mentioned. Although he still wasn't overly-excited about the project, he should at least view the land for himself, then he could decide if it would be a worthwhile venture.

Calvin sat in the passenger seat as the two men began the drive south. Dexter had programmed his car's navigation system, since he had no clue how to locate Peach Grove. In addition to seeing the land, Dexter wanted to get an idea of the town itself, given the fact a subdivision might be developed there.

He'd need to be aware of the amenities in the area, which were usually a vital selling point. In today's culture, most people wanted convenience, which meant not having to drive an hour to buy groceries.

The further he drove, the more rural the area became. If not for his car's navigation system, Dexter would be certain he'd taken a wrong turn somewhere. Had Randolph Waters been joking when he'd told Dexter's father about the land? The areas they passed through were a far cry from Fernwood, where homes or businesses covered almost every square foot.

He and Calvin had minimal conversation, which Dexter had anticipated, given the young man's quiet nature. After almost two hours of driving, they saw a sign that read, *Welcome to Peach Grove.* The sign appeared to be fairly new with peaches painted around the wording. Someone had obviously put time and talent into the sign, as it was pleasing to the eyes.

Just past the sign, a small diner sat back from the right side of the road. "Are you hungry?" He didn't miss Calvin's look of delight. Dexter parked his sports car, then headed into the restaurant. Immediately the aroma of cooking food greeted them, and the clatter of dishes and the hum of voices offered a casual atmosphere.

A waitress breezed by with a tray of water glasses. "Welcome to Retha's. Y'all just have a seat wherever you'd like."

Dexter spotted a small, empty table on the right side. That would be a good place to sit and observe the other patrons without being obvious. Maybe he could even overhear conversations to get an idea of the locals, since he was certain Calvin wouldn't be talking much.

The server who'd greeted them a few minutes earlier appeared at their table, smiling as she clutched a pen and small order pad. "Our lunch special today is the country-fried steak with gravy and three sides. What would y'all like to drink?"

After ordering their drinks, both men perused the

menu. Dexter was impressed with the offerings of this small mom-and-pop establishment. Not only did the home-cooking listings appeal to him, but there was also a brief background of the diner on the back of his menu. It seemed that Retha and her husband, Roy, had opened the eatery only five years ago, and from the looks of things, it was going strong.

Their server re-appeared, setting down their iced teas, a small basket with corn bread muffins and biscuits, and a small bowl of butter pats. "Have y'all decided what you gonna have?" The server, whose nametag read Layla, smiled at them.

After they'd both ordered their meals, Dexter commented, "Good thing we went ahead and stopped—it's getting crowded." Calvin nodded, his eyes following the stream of people at the entrance. Soon no empty tables remained. Impressive. If this was typical for the diner, then Retha and Roy had a booming business.

Calvin looked his way. "Seems to be a lot of farmers and repairmen."

"Maybe a few mechanics, too, if their clothes are any indication," Dexter said while chewing on a piece of ice. Most of the people appeared to know each other, with an occasional patron calling out to someone at a different table. At one point, a man called to another diner seated at a table fifteen feet away, as to whether the man's wife had given birth yet.

The man answered with a proud grin. "Nah, but we reckon it won't be long now." The man laughed and held up his cell phone, showing his friend he was prepared for the call.

About ten minutes later, Layla brought their meals. Dexter's eyes were bulging because the amount of food on the plate was enough to feed three men. After setting the food in front of him, Layla stepped back and smiled. "Hope y'all enjoy it, and if ya need anything else, just holler."

Their meals were delicious. After leaving the diner, Dexter followed the GPS directions toward the land. Hopefully it wouldn't be difficult to locate, since there seemed to be an abundance of land in this rural area. His mind flitted back to the patrons he'd observed in the small restaurant. What a contrast between those people and the residents of Fernwood. Especially the ones who frequented the country club.

Yet he had a feeling that the folks in the diner were good, hard-working people, and he had to admire that. He'd always heard that people who didn't have much wealth were often happier than rich people. That might very well be true because the jovial diners seemed to know and enjoy everyone in the restaurant.

Less than five minutes later, Dexter slowed his car and turned left onto a gravel drive. A simple *for sale* sign with a phone number underneath was posted next to the drive.

Calvin clutched his camera, commenting on the two-story house on the property. "You don't think anyone lives here, do you?" Worry tinted Calvin's tone, but

Dexter shook his head.

"I don't think so—it looks deserted." He shut off the engine, and he and Calvin climbed out of the car. Both men stood for a few minutes, silently gazing around at the land.

Dexter breathed in the fresh air. A breeze rustled the trees, and birds twittered from their branches. So peaceful and calm.

A sturdy wooden fence surrounded a large pasture, but no animals grazed within. On the other side of the house was a grove of trees, possibly a small orchard. Since Dexter was a city dweller, he wasn't sure what kind of trees they were, but they all appeared to be of one type.

Calvin had already begun snapping photos, so Dexter stepped forward to get a better look at the property. Was the house included with the property? Most likely so. An unexpected thought formed that he quickly filed away. This was such a lovely area that it almost seemed a shame to clear the land to build a small subdivision. He wouldn't admit that to his father, of course.

Fifteen minutes later, the men headed back to Fernwood. For a split second, Dexter was disappointed to be leaving such a serene environment and return to a busy area. Good grief. What was going on? Dexter Jennings had never been a fan of country anything—not music, clothing—nothing. So why did this area hold such appeal for him?

~ ~ ~

After arriving in Fernwood, Dexter parked at the real estate company, thanking Calvin for going with him and taking photos. The younger man appeared proud that he'd been asked to help his boss's son and thanked Dexter again for his meal at the diner.

When Dexter entered his father's office, Carl was scowling at his computer screen, shaking his head. "I was hoping our numbers would be higher in the third quarter, but I guess I'll have to be satisfied with these." He gestured toward his screen, then turned his attention to his son. "So, tell me about the land in Peach Grove. What did you think?"

Dexter chose his words carefully, because his father would surely wonder about him if he waxed poetic, describing the peaceful setting and the calmness that had come over him while there. "It's a nice piece of land, mostly flat, but with some gentle slopes. Enough to give it character. Some trees on the property that might be a bonus, since some buyers prefer trees on their lot."

"Hmm, sounds good. I'll be glad to see it for myself, but I'm glad you got a positive feeling about the land. We're planning on a two-street development, but this might end up being a three or even four-street subdivision. I don't want to get ahead of myself, since we haven't even purchased the land yet." His father laughed heartily, and Dexter could imagine the dollar signs flashing through his mind.

Minutes later, Dexter returned to his own office, hoping to make a few phone calls before his workday ended. But his mind remained on the Peach Grove land and how much it had appealed to him. Although he hadn't noticed any animals, the pasture appeared to be maintained. What about that house? Overgrown vines and bushes surrounded it, yet the house didn't look dilapidated. When he and Calvin had stepped onto the wide front porch and peered through the dusty windows, they saw empty rooms, but the walls and flooring seemed intact.

Why had he been so captivated by that area? Standing on that farmland, gazing across the property, and even enjoying a meal in the small diner had left him feeling refreshed. Maybe because farmland and small-town diners were not the norm for Dexter Jennings. He was a city-dwelling businessman, who thrived on the fast pace of urban life. Was it possible he might be changing? Surely not.

A little before five o'clock, Dexter decided to call it a day. He'd made a few phone calls but couldn't seem to focus. He chalked it up to the fact that he'd driven a total of almost four hours that day, not to mention eating that delightful meal at the diner.

On his drive home, Dexter stopped at an intersection.

A few women exiting a small building to his right caught his attention. The building's sign read *Manny Logistics,* and the women were apparently leaving their jobs for the day. One woman in particular caught his eye, and she was smiling while listening to a shorter, heavy-set woman walking beside her.

He couldn't pull his eyes away. The woman's long blonde hair hung loosely on her slender shoulders, and she laughed in a carefree way at her friend's comments. She was attractive, but Dexter had met more than a few beautiful women over the years, so he wasn't quite sure why she'd caught his attention.

The driver behind him lightly tapped his car horn, indicating the light had turned green. Embarrassed, he held a hand up in apology and pressed the gas pedal. Good grief. Pay attention, he silently scolded himself.

Dexter needed to pick up a few groceries, but decided to wait. His mind needed a break. He wasn't sure what had gotten into him, after being so drawn to the rural setting in Peach Grove, then sitting at a traffic light mesmerized by a woman he didn't know. Could he be having a mid-life crisis at twenty-nine? The thought almost made him laugh. He'd better not share these thoughts with Howard. His buddy would think he was losing it. And at the moment, Dexter wasn't so sure, himself.

~ ~ ~

Chapter 3

On Saturday morning, the butterflies in Claire's stomach forced her to have only one cup of coffee before leaving her apartment to pick up Marcy. There was no reason to be nervous, she'd told herself. Still, it was fear of the unknown. Not knowing what her inherited property would look like sent quivers through her.

"Are you okay?" Marcy questioned as she buckled her seat belt. She'd cast a curious glance at Claire as soon as she'd climbed into the car.

"Yeah, just feeling kind of jittery."

"Too much coffee this morning?" Marcy took a swig of her canned cola after she asked the question.

Claire laughed and shook her head. "No, in fact, I only had one cup, if you can believe it. That's why I brought this travel mug with me." She gestured to the tall insulated mug situated in the cupholder.

"Okay, what's going on?"

Claire knew her well-meaning friend was determined to get an answer, so she may as well open up. "I know this sounds crazy, but I'm nervous about seeing the property. I mean—what if it's swampland? Or what if people have been using the land for a dump, and I've inherited tons of garbage?"

Marcy burst out laughing, choking on her cola. After a few sputters, she drew in a breath and shook her head. "You're hilarious. Do you seriously think you've inherited swampland in this area of Georgia? I'm no geography scholar, but aren't swamps closer to the coastal areas?" Before Claire could reply, Marcy continued. "And I don't think people would dump garbage on a random piece of land."

Claire sighed. "I'm just nervous since I haven't seen the land yet. I've never inherited land before. In fact, I've never inherited anything."

Marcy reached over and patted her right shoulder. "You'll be okay. Here, maybe you need a sip of coffee." She lifted Claire's travel mug and handed it to her.

Claire took a big sip, knowing her friend was right. She was being silly and conjuring up ridiculous scenarios. Thankfully, Marcy changed the topic and chattered about the upcoming holidays.

Almost two hours later, Claire checked her car's navigation system. They were almost at their destination. Her pulse kicked up a notch as she gripped her steering wheel. She didn't want Marcy to regret coming with her, so she needed to rein in her nervousness.

Approaching a gravel drive, Claire slowed her speed and signaled, even though no other car was in sight.

Marcy squealed, causing Claire to grip the steering wheel even tighter.

"There's your house, and wow…it looks big. And there's a barn!" Marcy's exuberance reminded Claire of a young child in a toy store.

The house was partially concealed from view, situated about a hundred yards back. Claire eased her car onto the drive, her pulse pounding.

"Did you know there was a barn on your land?" Marcy's voice had risen an octave.

"No, the attorney mentioned a house, but he didn't have many details." Scanning the property, Claire didn't see anyone else, so she eased her car a little further, then stopped and turned off the engine.

After exiting the car, the women walked over to a wooden fence that surrounded a grassy pasture. "Looks like this pasture has been recently used. Did you inherit some animals too?"

Claire shook her head. "No, according to the terms of the will, I inherited the land and the buildings on it, which would be the house and the barn. But you're right—this does look as though someone has been taking care of this pasture." Before she could allow herself to dwell long on the field, she whirled around toward the house. "Let's head over to the house."

Marcy nodded, and the women walked back across the gravel drive and through the front yard. Although no recent landscaping had apparently been done, it still wasn't in rough shape as one might expect.

Stepping onto the front porch, the women paused to look around. "Do you have a key?" Marcy peeked into a dusty window.

"Yes, the attorney gave me one." She dug into the pocket of her jeans and held her breath as she inserted the key. The door swung open with a creak. This was surreal—was she dreaming? No, Marcy's almost-constant chatter reminded her this was all very real.

"Wow, this is amazing, Claire. It's dusty and needs work, but you could make this house beautiful." Marcy's face held awe as she gazed around at the large front room. She was obviously visualizing how the house could look, because she chattered on. "See that mantel? One day when you're married and have kids, you could hang their Christmas stockings from it. And maybe have your Christmas tree by this window." She gestured toward the large window overlooking the front porch.

Claire couldn't suppress a giggle at her friend's enthusiasm. "Whoa, girlfriend. Sounds lovely, but I'm not even sure I'll ever live here."

Marcy gave her a look that indicated Claire must be totally nuts. "Why wouldn't you? I don't mean right away but maybe one day."

Trying to keep herself—and her friend—grounded, Claire suggested they finish looking around. "I'm curious to see the upstairs."

Marcy nodded, following Claire up the wooden staircase. The banister was covered in dust, but otherwise appeared to be sturdy. While climbing the steps, Claire imagined the railing covered in Christmas garland. Good grief. Marcy's ideas were getting to her.

The upstairs level had four bedrooms and two bathrooms, all with windows that afforded a view of clusters of trees on the property. On one side, the two bedrooms overlooked what appeared to be an orchard, with trees that looked mature, but not ancient.

"Did you see the bedroom and bathroom on the first floor?" Marcy's excitement was obvious as Claire's head spun. This was all so much to take in. When Marcy began sneezing from all the dust, Claire thought it best for them to head back outside.

After locking the front door, she suggested they walk to the orchard area. Clouds had gathered overhead, and the earlier bright sunshine had dimmed. "Uh-oh, wonder if it's going to rain?" Marcy cast a worried gaze upward.

Claire nodded. "It might, so we'd better finish our tour and head back. Hopefully it won't storm on us, because I hate driving in a storm." She almost shuddered, thinking of a time in college when her car had hydroplaned. Thankfully no other vehicles were nearby on the road, but the experience had terrified her at the time, and to this day caused her to be extra cautious.

Moments later, the women jumped into Claire's car, snapping seatbelts, ready to head back to Fernwood. "Do you still want to stop and eat at that little diner we passed?" Claire tried to hold back a smile, because she already knew what her friend's answer would be.

Marcy bobbed her head and laughed. "Oh, yes. If that's okay with you. Sometimes those small, out-of-the-way places have the best food."

To Claire's great relief, the only rain they encountered on their return drive was a smattering of drops. Their lunch at the diner was delicious, and both friends agreed they needed to return there.

Claire pulled into Marcy's apartment parking lot. "Thanks again for riding with me. I didn't want to look at the house and land by myself."

"Are you kidding me? I was thrilled to go, and I appreciate your treating me to lunch. That was so good. I can't remember the last time I had meat loaf." Marcy eyed her thoughtfully. "Are you okay? You look kind of…" Her voice trailed off.

Claire laughed and supplied the phrase she was certain her friend had been thinking. "Out of it?" She grinned and nodded. "Yeah, I am. I still can't believe I've inherited something, and the fact that it's a house on an acreage just blows my mind."

Marcy reached over and patted her arm before climbing out of the passenger door. "Well, it's not like you were expecting that news. But this just might be the beginning of a big adventure for you." Her eyes widened and she smiled.

Later that day, Claire vacuumed her small apartment and tried to wrap her mind around the fact she was now the owner of ten acres of land that included a house and small barn. She needed time for it all to sink in before she made a decision on what to do with the inherited property.

She planned to phone her aunt the following day to share her news and ask for Molly's advice. Then she replayed what Marcy had said before getting out of the car that afternoon. Could this be the beginning of a new adventure? The thought was exciting and frightening, all at the same time.

~ ~ ~

On Monday, Carl met with Dexter to discuss their planned subdivision development. Dexter could tell his father was itching to start moving with the project and depending on him to make things happen.

About mid-morning, Dexter decided on a whim to drive back to the property. After all, it was a lovely autumn day and he didn't have any pressing business to tend to, although there was always work to be done. He told the secretary he'd return later that afternoon, then headed out.

While driving along the two-lane highway that led to the small town where the property was located, Dexter's mind drifted. What would it be like to live in a rural area? He honestly couldn't imagine, since he'd always been a city resident, much preferring the hustle-bustle of larger cities. Everything in this rural area seemed to move at a slower pace, including the man driving a pick-up truck in front of him. From what Dexter could tell, the truck was filled with assorted farming tools.

A few minutes later, the man eased over to the right shoulder and motioned for Dexter to go around him. Thank goodness. Yet as Dexter's sports coupe drove past the truck, the man grinned and waved a hand in greeting. Did the older man think Dexter was someone else? Maybe he was simply being friendly. Anyway, that was a nice gesture and enabled Dexter to pick up his speed.

When he passed the diner where he and Calvin had eaten, he was tempted to pull in, but resisted. No, he needed to stick to business details and investigate the property more thoroughly. Plus snap more pictures to share with his father. Calvin had done a great job with his photos, but it wouldn't hurt to have a few more.

Just as Dexter pulled into the gravel drive of the property, his cell phone rang, showing his father's name. "Hello, Dad. I just pulled onto the property, but I'll look around and take more pictures."

His father's tone indicated he was pleased. Carl Jennings had never been one to stall, and when he was interested in a real estate project, he went after it ful - force. Now he expected his son to do the same.

Five minutes later, Dexter walked slowly around the yard of the house, then ventured into what appeared to be an orchard. Maybe that could remain standing when the building commenced. It might even be an appealing selling feature to the prospective buyers, seeing an attractive grove of fruit-bearing trees on the property of the subdivision.

Twenty minutes later, Dexter decided he'd snapped enough photos and had also jotted some ideas about the street placements. He was getting hungry, but decided to wait until he returned to Fernwood to grab a burger. Easing onto the rural two-lane road, he turned right to head back to his office. Something was different, though, and a feeling nagged him as he slowly drove away from the property. Glancing in his rearview mirror, it hit him. The real estate sign was gone!

Maybe it had been moved. But he needed to know for certain, so when he reached the diner, he pulled in and circled around to return to the property. Minutes later his pulse raced. He'd not been mistaken, because there was not a real estate sign to be found. Had the owner decided not to sell the land? His fingers gripped the steering wheel as he exited the property—the same property Dexter and his father had big plans for, if they were able to purchase it.

While driving as fast as possible without speeding, Dexter tried to decide what he needed to do. Before he did anything else at the office, he'd phone the real estate number to inquire about the land. Again. But he may as well grab an early supper at a drive-thru before he reached his office. No sense in having to go back out again.

After paying at the window, he exited the burger place to return to his office. As he passed a two-story building, a blonde-haired woman was putting an envelope into a mailbox in front of the building. Dexter did a double-take and his heart raced.

That was the same woman he'd noticed the previous week. She obviously worked in the logistics building, because she'd headed toward the doors after finishing at the mailbox.

Maybe she wasn't even the same woman. Yet Dexter knew that wasn't true. He remembered her blonde hair and slender frame. Even the way she moved. *Get a grip, Jennings.* He needed to focus on business and stop dwelling on an attractive woman he knew nothing about. Absolutely nothing.

Minutes later he sat at his desk, his food untouched. Dexter knew he'd enjoy his burger more if he phoned about the property first. But after speaking with a realtor about the land, Dexter was afraid his burger would be a lead weight in his gut, because the news he'd received wasn't good.

~ ~ ~

What should she do? The question bounced around in Claire's head often. Every day. It had been almost a week since she and Marcy had visited Peach Grove, and it was finally sinking in that she owned ten acres and a house. Which meant that eventually Claire needed to make a decision. She didn't want to sell the property; of that, she was certain. Whenever she talked it over with Marcy, her friend's face lit up and she offered suggestions with exuberance.

On the first Friday in October the two women ate lunch at Skip's Pizza, surrounded by other customers and lots of noise. Marcy frowned. "Has everyone in town decided to eat at Skip's today?" She popped another pepperoni into her mouth.

"Yeah, it appears so." Claire took a sip of her water, then reached for her second piece of pizza. "When we leave and can actually hear each other, I need to tell you what I've almost decided."

Marcy's eyes grew rounder, and she stopped mid-chew.

Not wanting her friend to choke on her lunch, Claire went ahead and leaned in closer. "It's nothing major, just a thought I had last night. I'll explain when we leave." She grinned, then quickly changed the subject to the new décor in the pizzeria.

When the women exited the small eatery twenty minutes later to return to work, the early afternoon sunshine greeted them. Claire opened her mouth to explain her earlier thoughts about her inheritance to her friend, but abruptly stopped. A sports coupe, similar to the one she'd noticed a week ago, passed by. She focused her eyes on the license plate. DEX3 was on the tag, so there was no mistaking it was the same car.

"What is it? Did you see someone you know?" Marcy stood beside her, craning her head.

Claire shrugged. "Nah, I was just looking at that cute little sports car." She gestured with her hand in the general direction of the traffic light. Why was she reacting like this to some guy in a sports car? She knew nothing about him, other than his car tag made her curious.

Marcy didn't appear completely convinced but didn't press the topic. "Okay, now that we're not in Skip's with all that noise, please tell me your ideas about your property."

The women continued walking toward their building, but at a slower pace. "I've been praying about this a lot and can't help wondering if the Lord is prodding me in a new direction. Maybe I *am* supposed to move to Peach Grove and live in that house. But then I wonder…what would I do? It's too far to commute to my job here. At least for me that's too far to commute. Some folks drive hours each day to and from a job, but I'd go nuts."

Marcy nodded. "I agree. I don't understand how anyone does that. Life's too short to spend that much time in traffic. Besides, I'd become so stressed that I'd end up eating more." She sighed.

"So, I guess I'll keep praying for guidance, because this is a major decision. Besides, if that house sits there much longer, it'll deteriorate and require more than minor repairs." When she saw Marcy's impressed gaze, Claire shrugged. "My attorney said that, and it makes sense." She'd had the sincere feeling that Mr. Chadwick was trustworthy and wouldn't steer her wrong.

That evening at her apartment, Claire couldn't get the property and that house out of her mind. Truth be told, it was getting to the point where her inheritance seemed to consume the great majority of her thoughts. She plopped onto her bed and grabbed her Bible off the nightstand. Both her cats hopped onto the bed and curled up beside her. She rubbed their fur.

"I sure wish you guys could advise me. I don't know if we're supposed to stay here in Fernwood or move out to the country." Isaiah appeared to be giving her words some thought but then yawned sleepily. Simon had already settled into his usual curled-up resting position.

Claire smiled at her felines, then opened her Bible. Her eyes landed on two favorite verses in the book of Proverbs. *Trust in the Lord with all thine heart; and lean not unto thine own understanding. In all thy ways acknowledge Him, and He shall direct thy paths.*

No one else could tell her what to do, so she would continue praying and seeking direction from the Lord. He would guide her, she was certain. She just needed to trust.

~ ~ ~

On Tuesday morning Dexter arrived at his office earlier than usual. After the previous day's phone call, he'd muddled through the remainder of the day. He finally ate the burger he'd picked up on his way back from looking at the property again, but then regretted it.

He hadn't told his father about the phone call yet, but knew he must. Now he sat at his desk, a cup of coffee and his computer in front of him, but his mind was fuzzy.

All he could think about was his call to the realtor, learning that the property was no longer available.

"Dexter? Do you need anything?" His secretary stood at his door, eyeing him closely. She often arrived at the real estate office before he did but not today.

He shook his head. "No, but thank you, Dora. I came in a little early to get a jumpstart on today's work." He lifted the cup of coffee to let her know everything was fine.

Dora remained in his doorway. She clasped her hands in front of her and seemed to be contemplating something. After a few seconds of silence, she gave him a forced smile. "Were you not feeling well yesterday? I didn't want to say anything, but you appeared a bit unwell when you left the office."

For a split second, he almost blurted out the reason for his pallid and most likely pained face the previous day. But that wouldn't be a good idea, given the fact he'd not shared the news with his father yet. Instead, he mustered up a grin—albeit false—and nodded at the tactful woman.

"Actually, I was feeling a bit unwell. I'd eaten a burger at my desk, and it didn't set well. But I'm okay, and I appreciate your concern." Hopefully his explanation would suffice, although it sounded formal even to himself.

Dora smiled and nodded, telling him that if he needed anything to let her know. At that moment her desk phone rang, so she scurried toward her work area near the office entrance.

After a few more swigs of coffee, Dexter ran a hand down his face. What should he do? His father was set on purchasing the Peach Grove land, and Dexter had been certain they'd be able to purchase it and proceed with the development plans. Even if they had to negotiate with the seller, Dexter still was confident that the purchase would go through. Now he felt foolish, remembering how he'd stood on the property visualizing where streets would be, how the houses would look, and even thinking how the small orchard would add to the development's appeal to homebuyers.

His father's voice speaking to Dora jolted Dexter out of his thoughts. Why was he so nervous about telling his father? After all, he'd done nothing wrong. But he knew how Carl became when anything obstructed his project.

Might as well take care of this. Dexter left his office and stepped into the hallway to greet his father. "I need to speak with you, Dad, if you don't have anything urgent right now."

His father's puzzled scowl didn't help assuage Dexter's nerves at all. Carl nodded and gestured for his son to follow him into his office. Carl Jennings had the largest, nicest office in the company, which was appropriate. The polished mahogany desk was always in pristine condition, due to the fact that one of Dora's duties was tidying her boss's workspace each afternoon. Carl Jennings didn't like coming into a messy workspace in the mornings.

As Dexter lowered his tall frame into a chair facing his father's desk, Dora's footsteps indicated she was approaching, likely with coffee. Sure enough, she appeared at the doorway, holding a steaming mug of hot coffee. "Here you are, sir." Dora carefully set the mug onto the desk, asked if he needed anything else at the moment, and then left, sending a quick smile to Dexter on her way out.

Carl emptied the packets of creamer into his mug and stirred with the spoon Dora had brought him. "I feel very fortunate to have such a loyal employee as Dora. She's dependable and doesn't mind performing menial tasks. From what I hear, some female employees are insulted if asked to bring coffee to their boss." Carl shook his head in disgust, as though the very idea was ridiculous.

Dexter waited until his father prepared his coffee, took a sip, and then set it down. He needed his father to be fully attentive to this news.

"The reason I needed to speak with you is because I have some news." He paused, suddenly transported back to the third grade, sitting before the principal to explain how the ball he'd thrown had hit one of his female classmates hard enough to knock her down and lose her breath. It had been an accident, but Dexter felt guilty at the time, nonetheless.

Carl leaned in over his desk, his eyebrows furrowed. "Yes?"

Dexter cleared his throat. "I spoke with the realtor yesterday, ironically after I returned from viewing the property again. He informed me that the property is no longer for sale. The owner has decided to keep the property with no plans to sell." There. He'd said it, so now his father knew all their major development plans were for naught.

Carl scowled and shook his head. He lifted his coffee mug, then set it down again. "Was that all the information the realtor gave you? No mention of the owner wanting a higher price?"

Dexter shook his head and released a pent-up sigh. "No, there was no other information offered. Simply cut and dry. The owner doesn't want to sell the land."

Carl clasped his hands on his desk. With a scowl, he gazed intently at Dexter. "Anything can be bought for a price. What if we increased our offer?"

Obviously, Carl didn't accept the news his son had shared.

Dexter shrugged. "I received the strong impression that wasn't even a possibility because the realtor was quite firm about the owner keeping the property. I gathered there was no point in offering more money." Dexter almost held his breath, fairly certain his father wouldn't like his comments. Carl was used to getting what he wanted, even if he had to pay a higher price.

To Dexter's relief, his father didn't launch into a tirade about being a firm businessman and never giving up. Instead, the older man shook his head, then took a long, slow drink of his coffee. Silence hung in the air. After setting the coffee down, Carl looked directly at his son. "Okay, maybe it's just as well you didn't mention a higher price to the realtor, because we need to gather some specific figures first."

Dexter agreed with his father. There was no way he wanted to admit how drawn he was to that land and how disappointed he'd been to hear the realtor's update that the owner didn't want to sell, after all.

The men decided to discuss the matter at the end of the workday, after they'd gathered some figures and tended to other business. Dexter currently had two clients he'd been helping, so he didn't want to neglect them.

But for some unknown reason, he had great difficulty focusing on work that afternoon. His mind drifted between the land and his own restlessness. Maybe he just needed a break because he'd been working too hard. Wasn't that what his buddy Howard always told him?

Howard had also encouraged him to begin dating again, but none of the eligible single women in the Fernwood area appealed to him. In time, he'd find romance again—hopefully. He didn't want to grow old all alone. An image of a Scrooge-like character formed in his thoughts, and he almost laughed.

Okay, he'd make an attempt at dating again—when the right woman caught his eye. The image of the blonde-haired woman he'd recently seen twice flashed through his head. Yet what were the odds of seeing her again?

~ ~ ~

Chapter 4

Claire was eager to phone Aunt Molly, her late father's sister. Maybe she could offer some insight into what Claire should do, but first she needed to share the news of her surprise inheritance.

Aunt Molly and her husband, Ben, lived in Ellijay, Georgia, on a lovely, small orchard that sold apples and pumpkins every fall season. Although Claire hadn't seen them in months, they kept in touch by phone every week or two. When the middle-aged couple weren't busy with their orchard, they spent time with their one son and his family, and also were active in their church.

When Claire reached middle-age, she hoped to have her aunt's energy. She wished they lived closer, and now that she was facing such a major decision, Claire needed her aunt's advice. Her uncle's guidance, too. Though, she already had a feeling as to what they'd both advise.

Sure enough, after a pleasant, thirty-minute phone visit, Claire was more certain than ever what she needed to do. Both Aunt Molly and Uncle Ben had gotten on the phone to advise her, which she appreciated. That feeling of family connection offered a reminder that even though her parents were gone, she was not alone.

On Saturday, Claire and Marcy met for lunch at The Fernwood Cafe. As expected, Marcy was eager for an update. "Okay, so what did your aunt and uncle say about the property?" She leaned her elbows on the table.

Claire shared what her relatives had suggested, then blew out a sigh. But she was surprised at Marcy's reaction, because her friend appeared pensive. So unlike Marcy.

"Well, what do you think?" Claire wound a strand of blonde hair around her finger, a nervous habit she'd developed as a teen.

Marcy offered a weak smile and shrugged. "I'm happy for you and glad you were able to talk with your aunt and uncle. It's just now hitting me that if you move, you'll be so far away." A hint of moisture appeared in Marcy's eyes, and she grabbed up her cola, taking a long swig.

Wow. Claire didn't realize her friend would be so emotional at the prospect of a move, but it appeared she was. Who was she kidding? Claire would miss Marcy, too. A lot.

She reached across the table and patted her friend's arm. "Hey, even if I do move, we'll still be in touch. Our friendship won't change. You're stuck with me." She smirked, hoping to lighten the mood.

The server approached with their meals, which was a relief to Claire, given the fact her friend was acting somber. After a blessing for their food, Claire decided it best to change the topic, so she began chattering about Christmas. After all, she knew Marcy loved the holidays, so hopefully she could lift her friend's spirits by chatting about Christmas shopping, decorating, and baking cookies.

But later that day when she returned to her apartment, Claire was struck with the realization that if she actually moved to her property, her life would be vastly different. There was no doubt it would be a huge adjustment. With so much to consider, she needed to pray a lot more than she'd been doing.

At church the next morning, Claire and Marcy sat together enjoying the pastor's meaningful sermon. A thought occurred to Claire—something she'd not even considered yet. If she moved to Peach Grove, she'd need to begin attending a new church. With strangers. Tension ran through her, causing her to tighten the grip on her Bible that lay in her lap.

Okay, maybe she was getting ahead of herself. She hadn't made a definite decision yet but she'd have to look at everything that would be involved, including finding a new church home. Claire must have a place of worship in her life. Attending church was a necessity, as far as she was concerned.

Marcy must've sensed her tensing up, because she cast a quizzical gaze in her direction. Since the friends needed to remain quiet, Claire merely shook her head, hoping to reassure Marcy she was fine. She'd explain after the service.

When the friends chatted on the sidewalk outside the worship building, Marcy asked about the incident during the sermon. "I could tell you were gripping your Bible like a vise and was hoping you weren't in pain."

Claire laughed. "No, I wasn't sick, and I'm sorry you were concerned. I was listening to the sermon and suddenly thought about how it would be to start over in a new church if I move. And that's a big *if*, because I haven't reached a definite decision yet."

Marcy appeared to be giving her comments some thought. "Yeah, you're right. That drive would be too far to come back to Fernwood every Sunday, so you'd need to start attending a new church. Hey, remember that quaint little country church we saw? Maybe you could go there. *If* you do move. And I'll admit, I'd be happy for you to live in that amazing house, but I'd miss you something crazy. Especially at work and on weekends."

It was time to change the topic. She didn't want Marcy to get all sentimental on her now while Claire was already struggling with making the right decision. She tossed out a random question. "Did you see how cute Sami Henshaw looked today? She's over halfway through her pregnancy but looks wonderful."

Marcy nodded. "She did look cute. If I ever marry and have children, I'd probably just look fat during pregnancy." She shook her head.

"You would not. You'd look adorable." Claire hoped her compliment sounded sincere. Her friend struggled with her weight and would likely never be thin, but she had an attractive face and a great personality. She'd always tried to encourage Marcy but didn't want to sound patronizing.

Marcy grinned. "See? That's another thing I'll miss about us hanging out if you move. You always give me a boost."

Claire giggled. "That won't change if I move. We'll still have lots of phone visits, and we'll see each other too. Good grief, it's not as though I'd be moving to Alaska."

Later that day, Claire made a list of pros and cons about moving to her property in Peach Grove. That had been one of her aunt's ideas, which Claire appreciated. As she jotted her thoughts on paper, an unmistakable surge of excitement ran through her. Although such a move would not be easy, she was happy that the PROS list was longer than the CONS.

She'd keep praying about making the right decision but had a feeling she'd be phoning her attorney soon to notify him. There just might be a moving van in her future, after all.

~ ~ ~

Monday morning arrived with overcast skies—matching Dexter's mood. When he headed into the real estate office, the secretary greeted him and gave him one message from a client—cancelling a property showing scheduled for that day. He thanked Dora, then stepped into his office to begin working. Yet, he lacked the enthusiasm he used to have when he arrived at work. What was wrong with him?

Well, he needed to at least pretend to have his old enthusiasm because his father would surely notice and ask what was going on. The problem was—Dexter wasn't sure.

As though reading his thoughts, Carl appeared in his doorway minutes later. "Dexter, if you're not in the middle of anything crucial, I have some thoughts to run by you." His father stepped into the room as Dexter gestured toward a chair.

Thankfully, his father didn't seem to detect a lackluster spirit in his son but plunged into what he'd wanted to share. "I've spoken with several clients this morning, and one of them casually mentioned wanting to move to a rural area. When I tossed out the possibility of the subdivision we're wanting to develop in Peach Grove, the client was eager to start building." Carl leaned back in the chair and chortled.

Dexter's heart raced. Had his father forgotten they weren't able to purchase the property since the owner didn't want to sell? What was going on?

Carl shrugged. "I know the landowner doesn't want to sell, but we haven't been persistent. Yet. Dexter, I want you to phone the man you spoke with previously and tell him you'd like to meet with the landowner. Maybe if you speak face-to-face with the owner, he'll agree to sell to us. Especially when he finds out we're willing to offer more than the asking price."

Dexter's gut tightened. Sure, he could be persistent when needed, but practically demanding to meet with a property owner to convince him to sell? He wasn't sure if he could be *that* persistent. But when he saw the gleam in his father's eyes, Dexter had no choice. Carl Jennings had made up his mind that he wanted to develop a subdivision on that particular piece of land, and it was up to his son to make it happen.

Taking a deep breath, Dexter attempted to keep his tone calm. "Dad, I'll do what I can, but if the property owner is adamant about not selling, we'll have to accept it."

Carl stood from the chair and stared directly into his son's eyes. "I won't accept it until we've done everything possible, and that includes meeting in person with the owner of that land." The almost-smug smile on Carl's face indicated this conversation was over.

"Was there anything else you needed to share with me?" Dexter recalled his father had mentioned some thoughts—plural—he'd wanted to run by his son. Minutes later, Dexter regretted his question.

A wide grin spread across his father's face as he paused by the door. "Oh yes, there was. Randolph Waters phoned me about meeting for golf soon, and he happened to mention a surprise birthday party for his daughter, Brittany. It's the third Saturday of October. He and his wife want this to be a special event, so they're inviting numerous guests, including us."

Us? Dexter was confused. Mr. Waters wanted the Jennings family to attend?

"Yes, he wants the three of us to attend. We can ride together, if you'd like. I imagine parking space will be limited since so many will be attending. Be sure and mark your calendar. I've already phoned your mother so she could make a note of it. I expect this will be quite the event." Carl grinned and left the room.

Dexter remained seated at his desk, wondering if his Monday could get any worse. Already feeling out of sorts and then learning his father expected him to meet with the land owner to convince him to sell were bad enough, but now he was expected to attend a lavish birthday party for a young woman he cared nothing about? This was the proverbial icing on the cake, no pun intended.

The worst part of all of this was knowing that his parents had always expected him to marry into one of Fernwood's elite families, and now that he was approaching thirty, they apparently felt it was their duty to nudge him along. But what about his feelings? What if he didn't want to follow in his father's footsteps? Would Carl and Eve Jennings be shocked to learn that their son might decide to leave Fernwood someday?

~ ~ ~

Claire didn't know what she'd do without Marcy in

her life, not to mention her Aunt Molly and Uncle Ben. Their encouragement about making the move to Peach Grove was a tremendous help. Marcy's enthusiasm served to remind Claire that she was a true friend because even though Marcy would miss Claire, she still wanted her to be happy and do what was best for her life.

After much prayer, Claire decided this was the path she should take. Her uncle had even assured her that he and his son Jeff would take a look at the house the following weekend, making certain the structure was safe for her to inhabit. Claire had almost teared up hearing his heartfelt concern. She might not have a father on earth, but her uncle was the next best thing.

Claire decided to go ahead and speak with her boss about leaving her job, although she had no idea when she'd actually move. To her relief, he was supportive and assured her she'd be missed. The realization hit her. She was actually going to move from upscale Fernwood to a rural community almost two hours away.

While she finished projects at work Friday afternoon, Claire's mind buzzed with everything she hoped to accomplish over the weekend. She was excited about her relatives driving down to see her property the next day and couldn't wait to hear their thoughts. There were so many tasks to take care of if she was, in fact, going to move.

The ring of the phone snapped her from her mental to-do list. The attorney, Mr. Chadwick, was calling, and Claire had a sudden sense of dread. Had something fallen through? Was she not the owner of the Peach Grove property after all? "Hello?" She answered, hating the uncertainty in her tone.

"Hello, Claire. I hope this isn't an inconvenient time, as you're likely at work." The attorney sounded professional, yet there was kindness in his voice that Claire appreciated.

"Hi, Mr. Chadwick. It's fine—I can talk. I'm still at work but not in the middle of anything urgent."

He went on to explain there was a man who'd expressed great interest in purchasing her property in Peach Grove. "I kindly informed him that you were not interested in selling, but he was quite persistent. He even went so far as to say his real estate development company would go above your asking price for the land."

Claire struggled to process this information. Why would someone be so intent on purchasing that land? Could there be something valuable located in the dirt there? Nuggets of gold, perhaps? She almost laughed aloud at the absurd thought.

"Anyway, I wanted to make you aware of this. Now I am certainly not encouraging you to change your mind and sell. After all, the land and structures on it are now yours, so it's your decision what to do with the property. But being a man of integrity, I wouldn't feel right unless I'd made you aware of this persistent would-be buyer."

Claire didn't miss the fact her attorney had emphasized *persistent*. She immediately conjured an image of an elderly Scrooge-like character, seeking to accumulate more possessions.

"That's amazing that someone is so interested in that piece of land, and I appreciate your call to let me know, Mr. Chadwick. But the truth is, I haven't changed my mind about selling. In fact, I'm strongly leaning toward moving into the house not too long after Christmas."

"That's wonderful. I'm glad you're going to do that because this might prove to be an exciting adventure for you. I hope you'll be very happy living there, if you do, in fact, move." He paused and cleared his throat. "I do hope you'll stay in touch. My secretary, Mrs. Barnes, and I agreed you're a fine young lady, and we wish you the best."

Claire was touched by his comments and had no doubt he was sincere. After assuring him she would keep in touch, the call ended.

For a few minutes, she stared at her computer screen. It puzzled her as to why someone wanted to buy her property so badly. Sure, Peach Grove was a cozy little community out in the country, and there were likely many folks who tired of city life and traffic, and desired to move to a rural area. But the fact this particular person was willing to pay above the asking price of the property—if she was going to sell—made the idea all the more mysterious.

Oh well. No sense in dwelling on it because she wasn't selling the land. Or the house. Period. But she appreciated Mr. Chadwick contacting her. He must truly be a man of integrity, as he'd said. And Claire did plan to stay in touch with him and Mrs. Barnes. Maybe if she ever hosted an open house, she'd invite them. That thought brought a smile to her lips.

Before her thoughts veered off and she started planning an actual open house, she'd better complete her tasks for the day so she'd be ready to leave the office at five o'clock. Yet she couldn't deny the sense of excitement building in her. Maybe Mr. Chadwick was right, and this move would prove to be a new adventure for her.

~ ~ ~

What else could he do? Dexter had contacted the attorney about the Peach Grove property, and the man had assured him he'd let his client know that Dexter was eager to purchase the land. He'd stressed the fact that his company would go beyond the seller's asking price for the property—a tactic that often guaranteed a sale. Although in this case, the attorney had emphasized that the landowner had decided not to sell, and the man didn't offer any encouragement that his client would have a change of heart.

But he could hope, and that's what he would do. If he were on closer terms with God at the moment, he'd pray. But he'd pulled away from his faith roots in recent years when he'd become distracted with living the successful bachelor life.

To his dismay, Dexter couldn't stop thinking about

the tiny rural community he'd visited recently. It was almost like being in another world because Peach Grove seemed so vastly different from Fernwood, although the difference in miles was merely one hundred.

Now what to do about attending Brittany Waters' birthday party? Ugh. He did not want to go, but he had no choice—especially since his parents were also going. Why on earth were Brittany's parents wanting to make such a big deal out of her twenty-fifth birthday?

Howard phoned on Friday evening to make sure they were still on to watch a football game on Sunday. "Sure. Come to my apartment about thirty minutes before the game starts, and I'll order pizza." Before the call ended, Dexter was surprised when his friend mentioned spending more time with his girlfriend.

"You're still seeing Liz?" Howard had dated a woman named Liz a few times, but he didn't think the relationship would likely last, given Howard's past track record for dates. Yet, Howard's comments during their conversation now caused Dexter to wonder.

After the call ended, a melancholy cloud descended over him. Great. Now Howard would probably become serious with Liz, and before he knew it, he'd be attending Howard's wedding. That would leave Dexter as the last man in his small group of college friends to remain single. Which in turn would fuel his parents' comments about settling down. They meant well, but he didn't want to field questions about what he was looking for in a 'suitable young lady,' as his mother termed it.

He was beginning to wonder if there were any suitable young ladies available—at least in his part of Georgia. It was no secret his parents would be thrilled if Dexter married a daughter of one of their country club friends. But so far, none of them seemed right for him, including the one whose birthday party he would be attending soon.

For some unknown reason, the image of the blonde-haired woman he'd noticed appeared in his mind. That was crazy because he knew nothing about her. Yet there was something in the way she laughed at her friend's comments and smoothed her hair away from her beautiful face. He mentally chided himself. *You're twenty-nine, not in middle school.*

The next morning, Dexter headed to the gym, hoping a Saturday-morning workout would boost his spirits, but everywhere he looked, he saw couples. Cutting his workout short, he exited the gym and headed to his apartment to shower. Afterward, he'd do a little work on his laptop. Maybe that would keep his mind off of his pathetic single status.

But minutes later, the phone rang. His mother was calling to see if he wanted to join his parents for dinner that evening, unless he had a date. Some days, Dexter just couldn't win.

~ ~ ~

Chapter 5

Claire barely slept on Friday night. She was so excited about seeing her relatives again, and eager for them to see her property and advise her once they saw it. Butterflies swirled in her stomach as she nibbled at a piece of toast and drank some juice. Thankfully, the weather had cooperated, blessing them with a glorious autumn day.

Molly, Ben, and Jeff arrived at her apartment a few minutes after eleven that morning, and Claire had to blink back tears of joy when she saw them. She greeted each one with a hug, feeling a tug of emotion at being with her closest living relatives again. "How was the drive down from north Georgia? I hope traffic wasn't too heavy."

Uncle Ben emitted one of his hearty chuckles. "Nah, it was okay. Now if this had been a weekday, that would've been another story. You know Atlanta traffic is infamous in rush hour."

Claire agreed with him, again thankful that because she lived in Fernwood, her commute was short. "Now remember, after we look at the property, I'm treating y'all to a meal at the local diner in Peach Grove." She grinned at them, noting her cousin Jeff's eyes lighting up at the mention of food.

"Sounds delightful, dear." Molly flashed a sweet smile and the men nodded. "Are you sure you don't mind driving me while Ben and Jeff go in Jeff's truck? That way, when we finish, we'll head back to Ellijay and you can return here to your apartment."

"No, that's perfect, Aunt Molly. I'm glad to have you ride along with me—we can visit." She'd been looking forward to having some one-on-one time with her aunt, especially since her aunt was like a mother-figure to her.

The drive to Peach Grove passed quickly. Molly chattered about their life in the north Georgia mountains, and then answered Claire's questions about their family tree. In no time they'd arrived at Claire's property.

"Oh, honey…this is lovely." Her aunt exclaimed as Claire pulled into the dirt driveway, Jeff's truck following her car.

A tiny sense of pride filled Claire, although she hadn't done anything to earn this property and had yet to do the first bit of work on the house or land. But she had plans—projects she was eager to put into play. She turned off her engine and grinned at Molly. "Thank you. I'm becoming even more excited about all this." She gestured toward the house and surrounding property. "Sometimes I still can't believe I actually own a house and land. Especially after renting an apartment for so long."

The women exited the car and joined the men, who stood by Jeff's truck gazing around. Uncle Ben released a long whistle. "This is some spread, Claire-Bear. Lots of potential here. Before Jeff and I start checking the house, I'd like to walk around your property first, including that barn. You said you have ten acres, right?"

Claire nodded, not missing the impressed look on her cousin's face as he took in the sights around him. "Yes, the pasture area, the front and back yards of the house, and that small grove of trees over there. The best I can tell, those look like fruit trees."

Molly's eyes widened. "Yes, those are peach trees. That's appropriate since you'll be living in Peach Grove." They all laughed.

The women entered the house while the men walked around the property. Claire was surprised at how proud she was while giving her aunt a tour of both floors. Aunt Molly's positive comments added to Claire's growing excitement.

When they returned downstairs, the men entered the house. Molly immediately chattered about the interior. "Wait until you look around. This house has so much potential, and I can't wait to visit again after Claire has fixed it up. Oh my, how gorgeous it will be." She clapped her hands together like a young girl. Claire noted the amusement in the men's eyes.

"The land is pretty impressive too. You have more property here than I'd realized." Uncle Ben glanced over at Jeff, who nodded his agreement. "I know you told us ten acres, but once you start walking around, you cover more ground that it appears at first. That little barn over there is in pretty good shape, too."

Jeff's eyes widened. "Are you definitely planning to live here? It's your decision, but I sure would. I guess I'm a country boy at heart, though." He grinned sheepishly as his parents laughed.

Claire remembered that her aunt had shared a while back that Jeff had been saving money to buy his own acreage in the north Georgia mountains. She didn't miss the appreciation in his tone as he commented about her land.

After leading the men through the house, she stood with her relatives in the living room downstairs. Ben and Jeff both offered their thoughts on what they'd noticed and any obvious repairs that needed to be made. Claire listened in rapt attention, wondering if she should be taking notes. This was all foreign to her. But she needn't have worried, because her uncle offered reassurance as he patted her shoulder.

"This is a bit much for you to hear, I'm sure. But don't fret because I can ask around up in my area and see if I can find somebody reputable to do any needed repairs." Ben's determined tone was more reassurance for Claire. She wasn't completely alone.

"But since you're in the north Georgia area, would someone up there be willing to take on a job here? This is closer to middle Georgia." Claire nibbled her bottom lip.

Once again, Ben assured her that the distance wouldn't be that far, and he'd known of many workers who'd agreed to jobs out-of-town. "I'll let them know right away where your house is located, so they'd know what they're getting into."

An unexpected wave of emotion washed over Claire. She was so thankful to have such concerned relatives. It was obvious they truly cared. She blinked rapidly to keep any tears at bay, otherwise they might think she was losing it.

After thanking Ben and Jeff again for examining her house, she asked if they were ready to head to the nearby diner. Ben and Jeff both patted their midsections and laughed. Molly shook her head and chuckled.

"Those two are always ready for a good meal." The older woman grinned at her husband and son. Claire locked the door, still in disbelief that she was a homeowner. Minutes later they stood in the parking lot of Retha's Diner, the wonderful aromas beckoning them from inside.

"If the food tastes as good as it smells, we're in for a treat." Molly laughed as Ben held the door for the ladies.

"I hope you'll like it. I've only eaten here a couple of times, but it was delicious." Clinking silverware mingled with conversation and laughter greeted Claire's ears.

A smiling, middle-aged server approached them, holding menus and welcoming them to Retha's Diner. Then her gaze returned to Claire. "You've been here before, right? You look familiar to me."

Claire smiled and nodded. "Yes, ma'am. A couple of times when I was in this area." She didn't add that if and when she moved into her nearby house, she'd likely be stopping at Retha's often.

The group enjoyed a delicious meal while they talked and laughed. To Claire's relief, the entire conversation didn't center around her inherited property, but also included amusing stories from her aunt and uncle about their church activities and Jeff's job. Too soon it was time for all to head home, so Claire hugged each of them and thanked them again for spending time with her.

"Are you kidding? We enjoyed it, Claire. Besides, if I weren't looking at your property and enjoying this great meal, I'd be at home doing chores on the list from your aunt." Ben cackled as Molly shot him a playful frown and elbowed him.

After assuring Claire that they'd be in touch soon with information about someone who could do her repairs, Ben, Molly, and Jeff climbed into the pick-up truck to return to north Georgia. Claire slid into her car, waving goodbye and fighting the lump that had formed in her throat. She hadn't realized just how much she truly missed her relatives until today.

About to exit the diner parking lot, Claire's breath hitched as she noticed a sleek sports coupe signaling to pull in. The dark-haired driver stared at her, and their gazes connected, sending a jolt of recognition through her. She slowly headed out of the parking lot, but a quick glance in her rearview mirror confirmed what she'd suspected. The car's tag read DEX3.

That had to be the same car and driver she'd noticed in Fernwood, but what on earth would he be doing here in Peach Grove?

~ ~ ~

When Claire received another phone call from her attorney the following Monday afternoon, she thought he was simply touching base with her, as he'd done in the past. She was mistaken, and when she heard the actual reason for his call, her heart raced.

"I know you don't plan to sell your property, Claire, but that interested party is quite persistent. It might be best to go ahead and meet with him, so you can inform him that you are not going to sell. Period." Mr. Chadwick paused, then softened his tone. "I'm sorry to even suggest this meeting, but I've dealt with these determined types before. Sometimes my word isn't convincing enough, and they have to be told by the landowner."

Good grief. She wasn't upset at all with her attorney, just annoyed that a 'persistent party' as he termed it, was continuing to pester Mr. Chadwick. She drew in a deep breath and reluctantly told him that if it was absolutely necessary, she'd meet with the interested party.

"Even though I don't want to do this, I trust your advice. So just let me know what I need to do. And you'll be there too, won't you?" She must sound like a scared child, afraid to do something on her own.

"Oh yes, I certainly will be with you. In fact, the meeting will be held in my office but shouldn't last long." He gave her the information, assured her again there was no need to worry, and the call ended.

Claire quickly made a note on her calendar. She'd plan to leave work early on Friday afternoon and head to the attorney's office for the meeting. Hopefully he was right, and the meeting wouldn't last long. She was still mystified as to why someone wanted her land so much.

Marcy stuck her head in the doorway of Claire's office. "Need anything from the break room? I'm grabbing a cola in hopes the caffeine will keep me going." Before Claire could answer, Marcy frowned and stepped into the room. "Are you okay? You look a bit…flustered."

Yep, her best friend could pick up on her moods right away. Claire forced a smile and shrugged. "Yeah, I'm fine. Just received a call from my attorney about someone who wants to purchase my property in Peach Grove."

Claire stood from her desk, deciding maybe she could use some caffeine after all. "I didn't ask the identity of the person, but he's likely some wealthy land developer. I've changed my mind about coffee, so let's hit the break room."

The two women lingered a few minutes after getting their drinks, and to Claire's relief, no other employees were nearby. She needed to return to her desk and finish the current project she was working on, but wondered if she'd be able to focus after the attorney's call.

Marcy leaned toward Claire, concern etching her features. "What will you do if he offers you a huge sum of money for your property? Would you consider selling?"

Immediately Claire shook her head, almost spilling the mug of coffee she'd just poured. "Absolutely not. I've done a lot of praying and talked with my aunt and uncle a good bit, and I'm feeling more and more certain I need to relocate there. I'm even becoming more excited about fixing the house up and creating a nice home."

An unmistakable sigh of relief escaped Marcy's mouth. "Good. Because even though it's totally your decision, I've been excited for you. Thinking about how much you could do with that house, and all that land where you could take tons of photos. Even that little barn is cute. It's just such a peaceful, pretty area—not to mention that amazing diner nearby." Marcy giggled, her eyes glowing at the mention of Retha's Diner.

Claire couldn't help giggling with her. "Yeah, when I made a list of pros and cons of living there, there were so many positive things on my list."

"See? You're doing the right thing. Don't worry about that meeting, no matter how much money the person offers you." Marcy took a swig of her cola, and the two women exited the breakroom to return to their offices.

"Thanks, Marcy. You've really been a big help through this." She paused before adding, "And I might decorate one of my guest bedrooms at the house just for you. Then when you visit me, you can spend the night and have your own special room."

The squeal Marcy released caught the attention of a male co-worker headed toward the breakroom. He grinned and shook his head.

Back in her small office, Claire tried to stay focused on her work. She couldn't allow her mind to wander or she'd enter incorrect information into her computer. That could cause a huge mess, with all kinds of problems. No, once she reached her apartment that afternoon, then she could daydream about the big house she'd inherited and how she planned to decorate it. And she'd plan her approach with the interested party who wanted to purchase her property. It might help her nerves to have a small paper in her lap with some notes jotted down.

At least her kind attorney would be there, and he'd make sure the person didn't intimidate her. Still, she just couldn't shake the underlying current of nervousness at the thought of the meeting. *Focus on how beautiful your home will be when you fix it up.* She'd keep praying and try to remind herself she was doing the right thing. Hopefully, the person wanting to purchase her land would get over his persistence.

~ ~ ~

Dexter met with his father on Wednesday afternoon to discuss his plans. "I'm giving it one more try, and maybe this time will be productive." His father listened with a curious glint in his eyes.

"I must admit, son, that I'm proud of you for persisting with this project. Do you want me to accompany you when you meet with the landowner? Strength in numbers, you know." Carl rubbed his chin thoughtfully, as though planning a strategy.

Before his father jumped in and said he'd accompany his son, Dexter shook his head. "Nah, you don't need to, but thanks for offering. Besides, isn't Friday afternoon your meeting at the country club?" He smiled at his father, trying not to chuckle at the thought of the group of older men who enjoyed socializing at the club, under the pretense of having a homeowners meeting.

"Yes, but if I'm needed elsewhere, it's not a problem. There's nothing pressing on the agenda for this Friday, anyway." Carl glanced down at the large calendar he still kept on his desk. He'd refused to give in to technology and keep his engagements listed on his phone or computer. His father was insistent that he preferred to write his reminders in blue ink on the large calendar.

"Well, thanks, Dad. But unless you really want to go with me, I'll be fine. You keep saying I need to tackle more projects independently, so this will give me the chance to do so." Did he sound convincing? He sure hoped so.

As Dexter was about to exit his father's office and

return to his own, Carl stopped him with a question that sent dread running down his spine. "Have you purchased a birthday gift for Brittany yet? Your mother reminded me this morning that her party is fast approaching."

Drat. Dexter had temporarily forgotten about the birthday party that he—along with most of Fernwood's wealthy families—had been invited to attend. Forcing a smile on his face, he shook his head. "Not yet, but I'll get her something before the party. Unless Mom wants me to go in with you and her for a gift. I'd be glad to contribute some money towards whatever you and Mom are giving her." He should've thought of that sooner and mentioned it to his mother.

Carl raised a skeptical eyebrow. "That would be fine with me, but I'm certain your mother wants you to choose a gift that's completely from you. She thinks it would be more special." Okay, apparently his mother had specifically said that to his father, because there's no way his dad would be making that comment on his own.

Rather than getting into a debate with his father about his lack of interest in Brittany, regardless of the wonderful family she came from, he merely nodded. "No problem. I'll buy something for Brittany before the party." He returned to his office.

Doubts plagued him off and on the remainder of the day. Was he doing the right thing in meeting with the landowner? His father expected no less from him, so he had no choice. All he could do was make this final attempt for the land, and that was it.

But underneath his thoughts about purchasing the property and making his father proud, Dexter kept thinking about his recent drive to Peach Grove. When he was pulling into the diner parking lot, he was certain the blonde-haired woman pulling out was the same woman he'd seen in Fernwood. Why would she be in Peach Grove? Unless she had relatives there, which was a possibility. But why did he keep thinking about her?

Dexter wasn't sure what was going on with his emotions in recent days. The peacefulness he'd felt as he gazed out over the land in Peach Grove, and his ridiculous fascination with a woman he'd noticed in Fernwood and again in Peach Grove were muddling his mind.

Maybe his longing to keep visiting Peach Grove was due to the appeal of something he'd not experienced in his life. Always a city dweller, Dexter hadn't spent time in a rural setting, nor had he desired to. Until now. That land seemed to beckon him.

And the woman? In a way, something about her seemed to be calling to him too because if first impressions counted for anything, she was definitely different from the usual women Dexter was around. And in this case, different meant better.

~ ~ ~

Claire decided not to phone her aunt and uncle about her meeting with a would-be buyer of her property. No, she'd have the meeting, emphasize that she didn't want to sell her land, and that would be it. There was no sense in worrying Molly and Ben after they'd so kindly offered their advice and help. Not to mention giving up an entire Saturday to drive down from the north Georgia mountains to view her land. Besides, Uncle Ben had assured her that he would contact workers who might be able to handle the necessary repairs on her house.

My house. Sometimes when Claire thought about the two-story structure she'd inherited, not to mention the ten acres of land surrounding it, she could hardly believe it. Yes, she truly was a homeowner and a landowner. Exciting but also a bit scary. Actually, more than a bit scary—a lot scary. And the more she thought about it, the more she knew that house was where she wanted to live. She wouldn't even allow herself to think about a job. Not yet.

On Friday, Claire completed all her daily tasks at her job so nothing would be left unfinished when she left early for her meeting at the attorney's office. The day before she had cleared it with her boss, who thankfully didn't pepper her with questions. She also reminded Marcy, not missing how her friend's face filled with apprehension.

"You haven't changed your mind about not selling the house and land, have you?" Worry underscored her tone.

Claire shook her head. "No way am I selling. Hopefully this meeting will convince him I'm not budging." She almost laughed at Marcy's whoosh of relief. Then Claire continued. "I'll let you know everything that happens. Are we still on for shopping tomorrow?"

"Yes, and I can't wait. We can grab lunch while we're out, and you can share all the juicy details from your meeting." Marcy turned to head down the hall to her office.

Claire laughed. "I'm not sure how juicy the details will be, but don't worry. I'll tell you everything."

She sat at her desk to resume her work, hoping she could remain focused and enter the correct information into her computer. Then she'd leave and head to the attorney's office.

Finishing her work just in time, Claire shut down her computer, let the receptionist know she was leaving for an appointment, and hurried out of the small building to her car. She tried to ignore the butterflies skittering inside her middle, telling herself she'd eaten her small lunch too quickly. It was a wonder she'd been able to eat any of her salad, considering how anxious she'd been about this meeting.

Pulling into her attorney's parking lot ten minutes later, Claire gripped the steering wheel. This was ridiculous. She'd gotten herself worked up for no reason. It wasn't as though someone was holding a gun to her head, forcing her to sell her land. This was merely a formality, as her attorney had phrased it, to make certain the interested party received the message that Claire was *not* willing to sell her property.

A gust of wind blew as Claire opened the door to the lobby of the professional building. *Oh, great.* Now she'd look like a wild woman. Closing the heavy door behind her, Claire quickly smoothed her hair the best she could without a comb, noticing the receptionist smiling at her.

"Are you here to see Mr. Chadwick?" The middle-aged secretary asked.

Claire returned her smile and replied, "Yes, I'm Claire Durham, and we have a four o'clock appointment." She remembered the kind woman, Mrs. Barnes, from her previous appointment with Mr. Chadwick.

"Right this way, please." The woman gestured for her to follow, so Claire didn't bother to tell her that she remembered which office belonged to Mr. Chadwick.

She entered the attorney's private office, where he stood from his desk to greet her warmly. "Hello, Claire. So good to see you again. The interested buyer isn't here yet, but I'm glad you arrived first. The man seems quite determined from the impression I've received from our phone conversations." The attorney shook his head. "I'm hoping that by meeting with him in my office, we can send a strong message that you definitely do not want to sell. That *is* still your decision, correct?"

She released a nervous giggle, knowing she needed to control her jitters. "Yes, sir. I definitely do not want to sell my property. I've prayed about it a lot, not to mention discussing it with my relatives, and I know this is what I want to do. I'm keeping the land and hope to move into the house after necessary repairs are made." At that moment a rap sounded on the door.

Before answering it, Mr. Chadwick gestured for Claire to be seated. Then he opened his door to greet the would-be buyer, who strode in, seeming quite sure of himself.

Claire's pulse raced as she realized with startling clarity the buyer's identity—the driver of the sleek sports car with the DEX3 license tag! Her eyes widened.

He nodded and offered a quick hello, before lowering his fairly large physique into the chair that was only three feet from where Claire sat. She caught a whiff of his cologne—a pleasant, musky scent that likely cost more than she earned in a week.

Focus and be strong. She repeated the words in her head, then turned her full attention to Mr. Chadwick, who was making introductions. "Claire Durham, this is Dexter Jennings, the man interested in purchasing your property in Peach Grove."

Claire reached out to shake his large hand and a tingle rushed through her as their skin touched. Good grief. She must ignore the fact that he was so incredibly good-looking. And he wasn't even seated behind the wheel of his expensive car.

An undeniable look of surprise on his face caused Claire to wonder if he'd recognized her from the diner parking lot, but that was silly. Wasn't it?

Mr. Chadwick began their meeting and got right to

the point. Claire attempted to keep her eyes fixed on the attorney, but couldn't help eyeing the man seated close to her. He, of course, exuded confidence—the extreme opposite of what she was feeling at the moment. Deep breaths, she silently reminded herself—over and over.

When it came time for Claire to respond to Dexter Jennings's offer to purchase the property, she learned that it wasn't only he who was interested, but his father's real estate company. Hmm. Curious that they would so strongly pursue a plot of rural land. Maybe the elder Mr. Jennings and his wife wanted to build a country estate and retire there.

When her attorney and Dexter both looked directly at her, Claire pasted a smile on her face and shook her head. "No, I'm still not interested in selling my property. In fact, I've begun moving forward on my personal plans for the house and land."

She didn't miss the disappointment that flitted across Dexter's features, but he quickly leaned in with a wide smile. There was a look in his eyes that Claire couldn't quite discern—determination, maybe?

"Ms. Durham, after discussing this situation with my father, we're willing to offer you more than the original listing price for the land." He paused for a few seconds, then stated his offer.

Much to her dismay, her eyes widened again, and her mouth gaped open. "That's a very generous offer, Mr. Jennings, and I appreciate your willingness to go above the listing price of my property. However, it's still not for sale."

Silence hung in the air, but Claire plunged on ahead. "This property is more than just land to me. After visits there, I've realized I'm looking forward to relocating there in the not-too-distant future." She clamped her lips together, wondering why on earth she'd just volunteered so much information to this stranger.

Dexter nodded, uncrossed his legs, and rose from his chair. "I see. Well, I wish you the best, Ms. Durham. But in case you give it more thought and decide to change your mind, please know that my father's company is still willing to make an offer." He whipped out a business card and extended it toward her. "Just in case you do change your mind." His dark eyes bore into her face, as though trying to will her into changing her mind.

She took the card, hoping he didn't notice the slight trembling of her hand. The attorney had remained quiet through their brief interaction, but he also rose from his chair, shook Dexter's hand, and told him it was nice meeting him. Dexter shot one more glance at Claire, his eyes lingering a little too long on her face, then he exited the office.

Claire stood from her chair to leave, but Mr. Chadwick gestured for her to remain seated. She was secretly relieved because her legs were shaking, and she was afraid she might stumble.

He lowered himself into his chair and shook his head. "If you have a few minutes, Claire, I'd like to share some information with you." His kind, fatherly tone brought calmness to Claire's frazzled nerves, and she smiled and nodded.

Before sharing the information, he buzzed for his secretary, requesting she bring them a canned drink. "Or would you prefer coffee?" Mr. Chadwick asked gently.

"Cola is fine." Claire appreciated his kindness, wondering if she appeared as nervous as she'd been feeling. At the moment, she fully expected him to offer her a lollipop or sticker, just as the nurses had done after a shot when she was a child.

The secretary stepped into the office, handed the cold drinks to them, then patted Claire on the arm before stepping back out. Oh my. Claire must really appear frazzled to them.

She and the attorney both took sips of their colas, the coolness a balm to Claire's parched throat. She'd barely spoken during the meeting, yet was amazed at how dry her mouth was. Nerves, most likely.

Mr. Chadwick eyed her over the top of his glasses. "I hope this wasn't too unsettling for you, but I'm glad you were able to clearly inform Mr. Jennings yourself that you have no intention of selling your land. He needed to hear that from you. Additionally, you went on to add your future plans, emphasizing that you've no plans to sell. I'm proud of you." He grinned at her before taking another sip of his drink.

Claire had calmed a bit, but now was embarrassed at Mr. Chadwick's praise of her. Still, it was a good feeling knowing that she had someone supportive in this situation. "Thank you, Mr. Chadwick. I appreciate your support. I must admit I was shocked at the amount of money he offered. But I know I'm doing the right thing, and the more I've prayed and talked with my aunt and uncle, the more confident I am about my decision."

She paused, taking another sip of her cold drink. "As I mentioned earlier, I hope to relocate within the next few months, depending on how long the repairs take." Stating her plans aloud to the attorney somehow made things seem even more real to her. A ripple of excitement ran through her, whereas minutes earlier she'd only felt nervous jitters.

"I did a little background research on Mr. Jennings and his father's real estate company. From everything I've read and heard, they have a solid reputation, but are known for not giving up. Hopefully, Mr. Jennings won't persist in his attempts to buy your property, now that you've made it abundantly clear that you've no intention of selling."

"I hope not, Mr. Chadwick. Thank you again for your help—I appreciate it more than you know. If there's anything else I need to be advised on, please feel free to phone me." Claire stood, hoping she didn't pour the remainder of her cola down her clothes.

The older man beamed at her while saying it was a pleasure working with her. "I'm happy that you're planning to fix up the house and enjoy the land. And remember, if you ever have an open house, my wife and I would certainly enjoy visiting. In fact, to be quite honest, after I retire, we're thinking of moving to a rural area ourselves. Please be sure and let us know how you enjoy country life, once you get settled."

At that moment, his secretary tapped at the door to notify him of his next appointment. She smiled apologetically and whispered, "He arrived early and asked if you could go ahead and see him."

Claire was ready to head out, so she assured Mr. Chadwick and Mrs. Barnes she was leaving, then turned to thank him again. Exiting the building, Claire drew in a deep breath of the autumn air, overcome with relief that this meeting was over. A few leaves blew past her, and she felt she could float along with them.

Yet she couldn't stop thinking about Dexter Jennings. His gaze had lingered on her during the meeting, but it must've been because he kept hoping she'd change her mind about selling. There was no other reason he'd be looking at her so intently. After all, a handsome, wealthy man could surely have his pick of women. Besides, he likely wasn't her type at all. And she wasn't sure there was an available man who was her type.

~ ~ ~

After getting over the shock of realizing the landowner was the same blonde-haired woman who'd caught his attention—twice—Dexter focused on the matter at hand—her refusal to sell her land at the higher price he'd offered. She hadn't even wavered. His attempt to purchase the property failed, and his father wouldn't be happy. In fact, Carl Jennings would likely frown and tell his son he was losing his touch.

There was nothing else he could do. If Claire Durham didn't want to sell her land, she couldn't be coerced into selling. And Dexter sure didn't want another meeting in her attorney's office to try and persuade her—that was uncomfortable—a feeling he didn't like and wasn't accustomed to having.

No, Dexter Jennings was normally in complete control, smiling his way through many business deals and land acquisitions, then enjoying his father's praise afterwards. So, what was happening now? He'd encountered a situation where he had totally failed and in the process came out feeling ridiculous. He shuddered at the thought.

To make matters worse, the birthday party he was expected to attend loomed ahead. Brittany Waters would likely gush over him, and he'd be expected to return her affection. Never mind the fact that the woman did not appeal to him in the least.

When Dexter had returned to his apartment after the meeting at Mr. Chadwick's office on Friday afternoon, he felt restless, bereft. To his relief, his father hadn't phoned him, so Dexter decided to hold off on delivering the news. He was pretty certain his parents would be dining with friends at some point over the weekend, so hopefully they'd stay busy with their social activities.

Heading to the gym on Saturday, Dexter had a feeling of dread hanging over him. When his phone rang, he almost jumped. Ridiculous. Thankfully, the caller was Howard, confirming their usual plans for viewing a football game and ordering pizza. Exciting bachelor life, he thought as he clicked off his phone. At least he had his buddy to hang out with, or his life would be entirely lacking in the social area.

But on Sunday afternoon, his father phoned him. "Hi, son. Your mother and I didn't see you in church this morning, and she was worried you might be sick. I reminded her that you don't attend every Sunday." A wry chuckle followed his father's comment.

Ouch. He knew his mother preferred him to be in church regularly, but Dexter hadn't been on the closest terms with God in recent years, something that poked guilt at him often. After his disillusionment with Monique, Dexter had put distance between himself and some of the country club residents, most of whom attended the local church. It was a lousy excuse to skip church, but he tried to convince himself it was okay, since he attended now and then.

"Hi, Dad. No, I'm not sick, so please let Mom know. I was going to give you the bad news tomorrow, but you may as well know today. I got nowhere with the Peach Grove landowner, I'm sorry to say. She won't budge on that property, so we'll have to develop a subdivision somewhere else." He could hear the defeat in his own voice, and inwardly cringed.

After a few moments of silence, his father responded. "She? The landowner is a woman?" Before Dexter could reply, his father went on. "I see. Well, if you gave it your all, that's all you can do. We'll formulate another plan, but I won't lie. I'm extremely disappointed and had hoped we could develop that plot of land." A sigh escaped Carl's mouth, sending remorse coursing through Dexter.

"I tried, Dad. I really did, but she refuses to budge." The disappointment in Dexter's tone must've gotten through to his father, because the elder Jennings brightened and changed the topic.

"Okay, then. Moving forward, we have other clients to tend to, and maybe Randolph Waters will have a lead on some other property. Oh, and don't forget Brittany Waters' surprise birthday party coming up." As if Dexter could forget.

"See you at the office tomorrow." Dexter clicked off his phone, relieved that at least now he didn't need to dread delivering the news to his father the next morning. But as he sat numbly in front of his television, all he could think about was the beautiful woman who refused to sell her land. She didn't take the bait—not even for an unusually high amount of money.

Dexter wasn't sure why he continued thinking of her, but he did. It wasn't only due to the business meeting at the attorney's office. There was something about her—something he'd noticed in the brief time he sat beside her. An innocence that he didn't see in most of the women he'd been around. Certainly not in the women who frequented the social circles he and his parents were a part of. And for some unknown reason, that innocence appealed to Dexter. A lot.

~ ~ ~

Chapter 6

Driving to Peach Grove the following Saturday morning, Claire had a sense of anticipation welling up inside her. October sunshine streamed through her car windows and trees had gradually begun wearing their autumn attire of red and yellow leaves. Before she knew it, she was turning her car into the driveway of her property. *My property.* She was still adjusting to the very real fact that she was a landowner now.

Her gaze instinctively went to the right, where the house stood. Excitement surged through her. She couldn't wait to get inside, look around, and make notes of what she hoped to do to make the house livable. Of course, she wouldn't start moving anything into the house until all repairs and painting were finished, but she could go ahead and plan.

After climbing out of her car, her attention snagged on a sight in the pasture to her left. The fenced, grassy pasture that had been empty each time she'd visited was now occupied by animals. A lot of animals, nibbling grass or slowly walking around the pasture. Were they goats? She stepped closer to the fence that bordered the pasture and focused her eyes. No, these animals weren't goats. Or sheep.

Llamas! There were llamas on her property, and now a few of them had stopped munching grass to gaze curiously at her. They were probably wondering who the stranger was. Claire guessed the number to be about fifteen creatures. She eased a bit closer. Knowing nothing about this type of animal, she wasn't sure if they might charge toward her or even attempt to bite her hand, so she needed to be cautious.

She kept her eyes on the llamas and eased closer to the fence. They didn't appear vicious. Not at all. In fact, they were cute. Two of them even ambled toward her, as though wanting a closer look at this human. Were these animals included in her inheritance? Mr. Chadwick hadn't mentioned anything at all about animals—specifically llamas—in her inheritance.

"Hello, there. You're so adorable." Claire now stood at the fence, keeping her voice soft as she spoke to the two llamas that had approached her. It was wise to keep her hands to herself for now, although she had the tempting urge to reach over the fence and touch their fur. These creatures mesmerized her, with their brown eyes gazing at her and those cute ears positioned perfectly on their heads. Claire and the llamas continued staring at each other for a few minutes. Questions danced through her mind. Who did these critters belong to? Were they just here temporarily?

At that moment, the sound of a vehicle drew Claire's gaze away from her new furry friends. A blue pick-up truck had entered the driveway and stopped directly behind her car. Claire's heart raced, her old fears threatening to take hold. But she took a deep breath, not sensing danger from this visitor.

A middle-aged man in overalls and a ballcap climbed from the truck, his face wearing a somewhat sheepish smile. He hurried toward Claire and stuck his hand out when he was a few feet away. "Hello, ma'am. Are you the new owner of this property? I'm Boyd Felton, and my property is right down the road, headin' yonder. I see you've met some of my llamas." He gestured with his arm past Claire's pasture, indicating where his property was located.

The man seemed sincere, so Claire shook his hand and smiled. "Yes, I'm Claire Durham. I live north of Atlanta, but hope to move here in the next year. I like to check on my property when I can." She would never be rude but was more than a little puzzled as to why this man's llamas were on her property.

As though reading her thoughts, Boyd explained, "The previous owner had given me permission to let my llamas graze here now and then. Since it appeared no one else had taken over this place, I figured it was okay if I kept bringing them to this pasture." He hesitated, the sheepish look reappearing on his face. "I apologize if I overstepped, ma'am." He ducked his head slightly, then met her gaze again.

Claire had to fight the impulse to giggle, because he appeared so remorseful. She grinned at him and shook her head. "No need to apologize, Mr. Felton. I haven't moved in the house yet, and your llamas are welcome here."

Relief washed over his features and he beamed. "Thank you, ma'am. And please, call me Boyd. Around these parts no one is fancy. If you don't mind my asking, do you know when you'll be moving in? It'll be kind of nice to see someone living in this house again. I'd heard that the owner had rented it out, but then he passed away." He dipped his head in respect.

Claire had a feeling the owner he'd referred to had been her mother's half-brother, and again she regretted that she'd not known the man. She also had a feeling Boyd wondered how long his llamas would be allowed to graze on her land, and she wanted to assure him it was not a problem.

"I'm not certain exactly when I'll move in, but hopefully in late January or February. My uncle is going to oversee some repairs on the house before I move in, but please know that your llamas are welcome to use the pasture as long as needed." The surprise that registered on his face amused her.

"Why, that's kind of you. Thanks so much. They're really sweet animals and will help keep the grass trimmed in your pasture." He grinned again, then added, "I know my wife Maybelle will be glad to meet you." His gaze shifted between Claire and the llamas.

They chatted a few more minutes before Boyd Felton left. Claire couldn't resist speaking to the llamas before heading inside the house. She made a mental note to research llamas after she arrived back at her apartment, and also snap some photos of them. Claire was also eager to tell Marcy, who'd no doubt find this development funny.

With her spirits boosted even more after chatting with one of her future neighbors, Claire stepped onto the front porch and unlocked the door. She wanted to make the most of her time, so she whipped out her notepad and pen and began going room to room, jotting ideas about what she'd need and where to place the small amount of furniture she possessed.

From one of the upstairs bedroom windows, she had a clear view of the llamas. Captivated, she stood watching them for almost ten minutes. They were really cute and made a nice addition to her pasture. Maybe next time she'd bring her good camera to snap photos of them, rather than simply using her cellphone.

But for now, she'd better continue working on her decorating ideas and notes because the days were getting shorter, and she wanted to be in her Fernwood apartment before dark. Two hours later she had pages of notes and numerous ideas swimming through her head. When her stomach growled, Claire knew she'd better leave soon so she could pick up a meal at the diner and then drive home.

When she climbed into her car to leave, Claire

couldn't resist waving good-bye to the llamas, even though only a few of them looked her way. She hoped Mr. Felton would continue using her pasture because the more she thought about it, the more she liked the idea. After all, if she was going to live in a rural area, what would complete the setting of her home better than some farm animals on her property?

The thought almost made her laugh out loud as she swung her car into the parking lot of Retha's Diner. If Marcy had been with her at that moment, she'd be teasing her mercilessly about becoming attached to llamas. But Claire only saw this as another sign that she was, in fact, doing the right thing in planning her move to Peach Grove.

~ ~ ~

On Monday morning, Dexter entered his office with an uneasiness settling over him. Why was he feeling this way? No big appointments or meetings this week, only routine work and getting in touch with clients. His father already knew they weren't purchasing the Peach Grove property, so he wasn't dreading that conversation.

Then it hit him. Brittany's surprise birthday party was the upcoming Saturday. Oh joy. No wonder he had that uneasy feeling in his gut. Could he fake illness to avoid attending one of Fernwood Country Club's social events of the year? Doubtful.

As tempting as that would be, his mother was sure to

figure out what he was doing. Besides, he wouldn't feel right doing that. He had no interest in Brittany Waters whatsoever, but Dexter Jennings valued character, and being dishonest was not part of who he was.

He'd paste on a smile, take a gift, and show up at the party. Maybe he could stay hidden behind one of the large potted palms in the country club banquet room, where the party was to be held. Yeah, right. Brittany would hunt him down. Pushing thoughts of the gushy woman and her pending celebration from his mind, Dexter began his routine duties for that day.

Minutes later his secretary appeared at his doorway. "Come in, Dora."

The prim woman smiled and stepped a foot inside his office. "I, um…" Dora's smile widened. "I found out a little earlier that I'm going to have another grandchild, so when the baby arrives next June, I'll need to take some time off from work."

Dexter stood and grinned at her. No wonder she'd been looking so joyful. "That's wonderful, Dora. Congratulations to you and your family, and there's no problem about taking time off. When the date draws closer, you can just remind us and schedule your days off. I'm very happy for you."

She appeared pleased at his response and nodded. Still beaming, she returned to her desk. No doubt about it, Dexter had never seen Dora looking so gleeful, and it caused him to smile. He supposed a baby on the way affected people that way. Even normally serious folks brightened and smiled more.

Dexter was genuinely happy for the secretary. She was a dedicated employee, and Dexter and his father never had concerns about the woman being a slacker.

Focusing on the phone calls he needed to make that day, Dexter was moving in slow motion. There had been a time when he'd zipped through his duties with enthusiasm, tackling real estate projects and almost always being able to celebrate a completed transaction. Now he couldn't even convince a woman to sell her plot of land in a rural area. Discouragement combined with thoughts of the beautiful landowner waged a battle in his mind.

Good grief! What was wrong with him? He wasn't in middle school again, harboring a secret crush on the prettiest cheerleader. Yet there was no denying that he found Claire more than a little attractive, and the more he thought about her, the more he couldn't deny that he'd like to know more about her. Even if she wasn't willing to sell her land.

Reaching for a folder, Dexter returned to the news Dora had shared. A baby on the way. Would he ever experience that for himself? His parents had made no secret about the fact they would absolutely love to be grandparents someday. And he wasn't getting any younger. But that would require marriage, and Dexter had yet to meet a woman he loved enough to marry.

For reasons he didn't care to examine, Dexter's mind again flashed to an image of Claire. The breeze lifting her blonde tresses from her shoulders. Her pretty face as she'd laughed at comments made by a friend. Then seated a mere two feet away in the attorney's office, when Dexter had attempted to purchase her property—and failed.

Something about her intrigued him, and that thought concerned him. There were more than a few women in the Fernwood area who'd gladly date him, but so far none of them appealed to him. Especially not the woman he'd be attending a birthday party for in a few days. A heaviness settled in his gut, making the doughnut he'd eaten feel like an anchor.

No way was he interested in Brittany Waters. It didn't matter how wealthy her family was or how much his parents would enjoy seeing him and Brittany together. After all, didn't his happiness count for something?

~ ~ ~

"Yes, Aunt Molly—llamas! And they are adorable." Claire had phoned her aunt and uncle on Monday evening to say hello and let them know she'd visited her property again. She'd also been eager to tell them about the llamas who sometimes grazed in her pasture. After chatting with her aunt for a bit, Claire spoke with her uncle, thanking him again for his help.

"I have some good leads on workers for the repairs and painting. I just hope you weren't counting on being in your house by Christmas." Uncle Ben's words made Claire laugh. She'd be a total basket case if she'd planned to move before Christmas—especially since they were well into October.

"No worries, Uncle Ben. I'll be thankful if I'm moved in by early springtime of next year. The work will take time, and I've still got a lot to do. Not to mention finishing all my projects at work."

She didn't miss the relief in her uncle's tone, and they talked a few more minutes about the various tasks to be done on her house. They agreed it was better to get as much done before Claire actually moved into the house.

After she clicked off her phone, her thoughts returned to the llamas. When she'd told Marcy about seeing them, her friend had shared her enthusiastic feeling. "I can't wait to see them. Maybe the next time I visit your land with you, the llamas will be grazing." Marcy's comments fueled Claire's excitement over the animals, in addition to tamping down her anxious thoughts about finding a job in Peach Grove. She refused to fret about that just yet.

With her mind whirling with happy thoughts about the Peach Grove house and the llamas, Claire had difficulty settling down to sleep. She'd likely be groggy the next morning, and it would only be Tuesday.

Sure enough, when her alarm sounded, Claire's head throbbed from too little sleep, but she pushed herself out of bed and got ready for work. Hopefully her mug of coffee would help. After feeding her cats, she grabbed her bag, keys, and coffee, and headed out. Why couldn't today be Friday? Then at least she could catch up on sleep over the weekend.

Driving into the Fernwood business district, Claire wondered why the traffic was especially heavy that morning. It wasn't long before she saw the reason for the congestion. One of the main intersections had a non-functioning traffic light. Apparently, the problem had recently happened because Claire didn't notice any police in the area to direct traffic and keep everyone moving.

When Claire reached the intersection, she waited for her turn to ease forward. Just as she reached the middle of the intersection, a jarring crash sounded, and her body jolted forward. With her throbbing head and now-aching upper torso, Claire sat, dazed at the realization that another driver had just slammed into her car. This was *not* the way she'd hoped her day would begin.

"Ma'am, are you okay? I'm so sorry I hit you. My parents are going to be so mad at me. Are you okay?" The teen-aged girl didn't appear hurt at all, but she was more than a bit upset. She crouched down outside of Claire's car window and stuck out a trembling hand to open the door.

Thankful that her vehicle door still worked, Claire helped push it open before gingerly climbing out of her car. Apparently as she'd felt the impact, her body had tensed, judging from the soreness she now had. The young girl, still sobbing, grabbed Claire in an embrace as she continued apologizing.

Over the girl's shoulder, Claire could see a few people who'd gathered around, including a policeman hurrying toward them. But one face in particular drew her focus more than the others. A man with lines of worry etched into his handsome features stepped toward her. Dexter Jennings. What on earth was he doing here?

Claire needed to comfort the young girl and assure her things would be okay. Taking in the scene around her, this fender-bender had caused quite a mess for many drivers. Claire patted the girl's arm. "I'm okay, I promise. I'm not hurt, just a little sore. Are you injured?"

The girl shook her head, then wiped her nose on her sleeve. Somehow, Claire had grabbed her handbag before climbing from her car, and now numbly reached inside for a tissue for the girl. "Here, use this. I promise I'm fine."

With a shaky nod, the girl mustered a weak smile and took the tissue, wiping her nose through her sniffling. The police had reached them and was writing down an account of what happened. Claire hadn't been at fault and wasn't sure why the teen had hit her, but she was thankful for the police presence so this could be cleared up. She'd never been so ready to reach her office and be seated at her computer desk.

The policeman was kind but professional, instructing the passers-by to continue on their way and telling Claire and the teen where to move their cars before he spoke with each of them again. As she climbed back into her car to pull it into a parking space fifty yards ahead, Dexter reached her.

"Claire? Are you okay? I was heading into my office just as this happened. Then I realized you were one of the people involved. Can I do anything for you?" Genuine concern shone in his dark eyes. As he leaned in her car window, a whiff of his musky cologne reached Claire's nose, offering a pleasant smell in direct contrast to the gasoline fumes surrounding them.

She managed a shaky smile. "Thank you, but I'm okay. Just very thankful the Lord was watching over me and that young girl so there were no injuries. I'm a bit sore but no big deal." The policeman was waiting for her to move her car so she needed to get going. "I'd better move since we're blocking this intersection."

After a quick nod, Dexter stepped over to the sidewalk. Was he waiting on her? Shouldn't he be heading to his job now that he'd seen there were no injuries? Surely, he wasn't going to use the opportunity to convince her to sell her Peach Grove property. Was he?

Slowly easing her now-dented car forward, Claire parked in the spot the policeman had indicated, then stepped out, with her handbag still draped on her shoulder. Sure enough, Dexter stood on the sidewalk, as though waiting to make sure all was well. She'd like to think he was doing this because he truly had a good heart, but she still had that wealthy realtor image in her head, so she wasn't taking any chances.

Twenty minutes later the policeman finished examining the cars, questioned both women, and handed the teen a ticket. She accepted it with a guilty expression and tears still lingering in her eyes.

"I should've been paying attention. I only looked at my radio for a second and didn't think about it being my turn to stop at the intersection." She'd already given her insurance information to Claire, and both women had assured the policeman they didn't need an ambulance.

The middle-aged police stood for a few minutes, lecturing the teen in a stern but fatherly manner. "This could've been much worse, young lady. I hope you'll see this as a lesson so it won't happen again."

She assured him she'd be more careful, then hugged Claire again before heading to her damaged car. Exhaustion crept over Claire. She turned to head back to her car and continue to work. Thankfully she'd sent a quick text to Marcy about running late, but didn't specify the reason so as not to alarm her best friend. Marcy would let their boss know.

Dexter intercepted Claire as she reached her car. Why was he still here? He grinned, his dark eyes gazing at her, as though wanting to know her thoughts. "Are you sure you're okay? Even a fender bender can cause injuries." His eyes now traveled down to her feet as she climbed inside her car.

"I'm fine, really. I just hadn't planned on my day starting this way." A feeble laugh came out, and she shook her still-throbbing head. "Thank you for checking on me, though. I appreciate it and know you need to get to work. I'm headed to my job now." She didn't want to be rude, but desperately needed to be in her office with two headache tablets, washed down with a strong mug of coffee.

He apparently received the message, because he nodded and added another comment about being relieved she wasn't hurt. "Well, have a good day. At least it can only get better, right?" He grinned and winked, sending a spark running through Claire.

When she arrived at her office minutes later, she was wiped out. Her workday hadn't even begun, and she was already tired. But she wouldn't give in to the urge to return to her apartment and take a nap. No, she'd put in a full day, making up for her late arrival time. Marcy would be shocked when she learned what had happened that morning. And her friend would be just as shocked that the handsome real estate agent had stopped to check on her and then hung around.

On second thought, maybe she'd better leave off the details about Dexter. Knowing Marcy, she'd read something into that. And there was nothing to read into it—a simple act of kindness—nothing more. Claire wasn't sure if that disappointed her or not.

~ ~ ~

When Dexter had been about to enter his father's real

estate company that morning, he heard a crashing sound, and froze. That ominous sound jerked his thoughts back to an accident he'd been involved in as a teen. One that had changed his driving habits for the better. Thankfully there had been no serious injuries in that incident, and Dexter hoped the same for whatever had just happened.

His curiosity tweaked when he saw two vehicles in the middle of the intersection, the flashing yellow traffic light indicating it wasn't working properly. Good grief. Some driver hadn't waited their turn before heading through the intersection. So dumb.

But as he'd approached the scene, he recognized the woman standing beside her car, with a young girl sobbing on her shoulder. Claire Durham! Dexter ended up staying near the accident scene to ensure that she was okay. He didn't miss the surprised glint in her eyes when she'd seen him.

Although Dexter had felt slightly awkward when speaking to her afterward, Claire seemed to appreciate his concern. At least, he *hoped* she did. He was sincere in wanting to make certain she was okay, even though the damage to her car wasn't too bad.

Now sitting at his desk, he couldn't stop thinking about her. Even after she'd been hit in her car and was no doubt shaken up, the woman was still beautiful. Not in a flashy way, as most of the women from his country club environment were, but in a kind, gentle way. Her mannerisms accentuated her beauty. Watching her hand a tissue to the distraught teen who'd rammed her car evidenced a true act of caring.

When his father appeared at his doorway minutes later, it was a wake-up call to get busy. He shouldn't be sitting here, daydreaming about someone he longed to know better, but rather working on real estate business.

"Do you have a minute, Dexter?" The serious gaze his father sent him caused Dexter to go on alert. Had something happened with one of their clients?

Dexter nodded. "Sure, Dad." He gestured toward one of the chairs.

Carl rubbed a hand over his face and shrugged. "Well, as much as I'd hoped to buy that piece of land in Peach Grove, maybe it's just as well it didn't work out. Your mother has been after me to retire so we can travel." He paused and shook his head. "The traveling part sounds good, but I've been working here for so long…it's hard for me to think of being retired."

His father's talk about retirement shouldn't come as a surprise to Dexter, but it still caught him off guard. Now as he studied his father closely, Dexter noticed a tiredness in his features. His dad had gained some weight. Maybe retirement *would* be good for him.

"It would be a major change, but think of how much fun you and Mom would have traveling and doing things you both enjoy." *Besides dining and socializing at the country club.* Dexter kept that thought to himself.

Carl shrugged. "Yes, I'm sure there would be advantages to not having to run this real estate office any longer. Which brings me to the other matter I wanted to mention." He paused and gazed directly at his son. "Are you interested in taking over the company? When you first began your career, you'd talked as though that was your plan when I retired. But in the past year, I've had the impression that maybe you were having second thoughts." His father's tone held no judgment, but he'd gotten directly to the point.

Dexter should've known this conversation was bound to happen soon—he just didn't think it would happen that day. He gathered his thoughts and chose his words carefully. "Dad, I'm not sure. As your only son, it would make sense for me to continue on here, but…" His voice trailed off as he attempted to think of how to word his feelings without hurting his father.

Carl stood from his seat and offered a weak smile to Dexter. "I don't need to know right now. But just think about it, so we can have details in place before my actual retirement. At this point, I'm thinking I should work at least another year or so." He paused and winked. "But don't tell your mother. She's counting on my retiring sooner." With a tired-sounding chuckle, his father ambled out of the room toward his own office.

At least his father hadn't pressured him for a decision right away, because the truth was, Dexter didn't know what he wanted to do. Real estate was a career he'd enjoyed at times, but over the past year, he'd begun having some doubts, as though maybe there was something else he was better suited for. The problem was, he had no idea what that job would be.

~ ~ ~

When Saturday arrived, Dexter awoke with a headache. Yet if he phoned his parents to say he wasn't attending Brittany's surprise party, they'd be disappointed. And possibly upset. His mother would likely suspect that he was looking for an excuse to get out of attending. She would be right, of course.

After guzzling coffee and taking a headache tablet, Dexter phoned his parents to see what time he should pick them up. He'd insisted on the three of them riding to the country club together, because then there was no way he could be railroaded into taking Brittany on a date after her party.

Howard phoned him around noon. "Is today the big party?"

Dexter groaned. "Yes, and I'll be glad when it's over. You want to come over this evening to watch the game? I could pick up food or order pizza."

Normally, Howard would respond right away in an eager tone, but this time there was silence. After a few seconds he explained he had a date with Liz. His less-than-enthusiastic voice sparked curiosity in Dexter.

"Okay, we'll watch a game another weekend. What are you and Liz doing?" Dexter couldn't help wondering why Howard kept seeing the woman now and then if he wasn't interested.

"I'm taking her to that French restaurant that opened

up a while back."

"Oh, fancy." Dexter laughed, not hearing any laughter in return. Okay, apparently Howard was not thrilled about his date.

"Yeah, she's been wanting to eat there, so I figured we'd give it a try. I just hope it's not too pricey."

"You'll have to let me know how it is. Uh oh, my mom is phoning so I'd better catch her call. We're supposed to ride together to the party."

"Have fun." Howard's flat tone summed up the way Dexter felt. He switched over to answer her call.

"Hello, dear. Just wanted to remind you I have a lovely gift bag for you to use for Brittany's present. You said you bought her a gift card, so when you arrive at our house, you can place the card in the bag. I also have some color-coordinated tissue paper to fill it."

Dexter couldn't help grinning at his mother's words. She still spoke to him as though he was a young kid, but he never complained to her. It was her mothering instinct.

"Thanks, Mom. I'll pick you and Dad up at four-thirty, as we planned."

A few hours later, Dexter and his parents arrived at the Fernwood Country Club, gifts in tow. It appeared most of the other attendees hadn't yet arrived because only a handful of people milled about the large banquet room.

When Brittany's parents saw the Jennings family enter, they rushed over to greet them. Lucinda Waters grabbed Dexter's hands. "Brittany will be thrilled y'all are here. Especially you, Dexter." The woman's eyes sparkled as much as the jewelry she wore.

Were those diamonds and emeralds real? Dexter couldn't help noticing her rings as she released his hands and gestured dramatically while speaking. Not to mention her necklace and earrings.

"Everything's ready—the caterer has a lavish buffet planned, and our DJ is ready with music that will appeal to the younger attendees in addition to the older ones." Lucinda smiled demurely at Dexter's parents.

Carl Jennings and Randolph Waters were soon engaged in business-related conversation while Dexter's mom and Lucinda chatted about the party decorations. Dexter stood off to the side, nervously glancing around to see if anyone else in his age group had arrived yet. No, at the present time, the attendees all looked to be friends of Brittany's parents. Surely, they'd invited Brittany's friends. His palms began to sweat. This was absurd—he was almost thirty, not to mention a successful businessman.

Thankfully, minutes later a few young women arrived, followed by a man who obviously was the date for one of them. Dexter recognized two of the women from the community but didn't actually know them.

Lucinda tapped a spoon against a glass to get the group's attention. "Okay, everyone. Time to shout 'surprise' when Brittany enters. Her brother is bringing her in about five minutes. Thank you to all who are here—I'm sure this will mean so much to our Brittany." Her eyes lingered on Dexter, giving him the urge to crawl underneath one of the linen-covered tables.

He'd have to speak to the guest of honor and wish her a happy birthday, but he hoped others would also be speaking to her, so it wouldn't be awkward. How he wanted this party to end.

When Brittany entered, everyone shouted in excited tones, along with some cheering and clapping. The birthday honoree widened her eyes and placed her well-manicured hands to her cheeks. Her expression of being surprised had to be completely fake. Dexter felt a bit guilty for thinking that, but it was true. The way she batted her eyes, gasping as she gazed around the room, almost sent a wave of nausea through Dexter.

Okay, hopefully the food would be good, and his parents wouldn't want to linger here too long. There were other ways he'd prefer to spend a Saturday, and none of them involved watching Brittany Waters greeting her guests in a forced show of appreciation.

When she reached the table where Dexter and his parents sat, along with an older couple, Brittany spoke to the others first before stopping at Dexter's chair, reaching down and clasping his arm. "It's so good to see you, Dexter. Why don't you sit at my table?" She batted her eyes so much that Dexter was certain her artificial eyelashes would drift down to his lap.

"Well, I…uh, my parents—" Before he could complete his shaky sentence, his mother leaned over, smiling and encouraging him to go and sit with Brittany. *Thanks, Mom.* He was twenty-nine years old, but at the moment felt as though he was in pre-school, being encouraged to join his playmates.

How could this be happening? All he'd wanted to do was make an appearance at this party to be polite—and please his parents. No way had he planned on being paired with Brittany. His gut clenched. Hopefully, her girlfriends would chat with her, and Dexter could at least enjoy the food. At that moment, Brittany's parents spoke to the guests, who appeared to be around fifty, from what Dexter counted.

"Thank you all for joining us to celebrate our baby girl's twenty-fifth birthday. After our pastor blesses the food, we'll let Brittany and her table go first in the buffet line. Everyone enjoy yourselves, and after the meal, we'd love to see many of you on the dance floor." Lucinda finished her spiel, then the pastor offered a blessing.

Somehow Dexter enjoyed his meal and only had minimal conversation with the others at his table, including Brittany. Now if he could get through the rest of this ordeal and leave, he'd be happy. But no, it wasn't that simple. About ten minutes after eating, Brittany insisted that Dexter dance with her. With pouty lips and wide eyes, she gazed up at him.

"It wouldn't be right if I didn't dance. After all, I'm the birthday girl." She emitted a giggle that sounded forced, and Dexter wanted to gag. Could she be any more immature? Since he had no choice, he accompanied her to the dreaded dance floor, hoping to blend in with the others.

As expected, his mother again beamed at him, no doubt already planning a wedding for Dexter and Brittany in her mind. No. Way. Before he would consent to marrying someone phony, not to mention the fact she didn't appeal to him at all, he'd remain single. Forever.

After several tortuous tunes on the dance floor, he'd had enough. Dexter rubbed his forehead and frowned, then leaned over to Brittany so she could hear him above the DJ's voice and the attendees. "I'm going to need to take a break. My head is hurting, so you might want to find another dance partner." He said it kindly, but Brittany's eyes flashed in indignation.

He hurried to his parents' table to discreetly tell them he was ready to leave, much to his mother's dismay. She must've seen the determination in his eyes because she didn't argue. His father wrapped up a conversation he'd been having with another man, then they headed toward the door.

Wanting to do the right thing, Dexter stepped over to Brittany, who was chatting with an older couple near her table and told her he had a nice time. As expected, her face morphed into a pout at his words.

Brittany turned her full attention on Dexter. "You're leaving now? My party has barely begun." Her high-pitched voice reminded him of a spoiled child.

To his relief, his parents stepped beside him,

showering Brittany with kind comments about how pretty she looked. Their compliments seemed to soften her, at least a little. Dexter gripped his car key, eager to make an exit.

Minutes later, he and his parents were in the country club parking lot, heading toward Dexter's car. As expected, his mother had a few choice words ready for him. "Really, Dexter. Couldn't we have stayed a while longer? Your father and I could have easily gotten a ride home with one of the other attendees so you could've stayed and spent time with Brittany."

By this point, his headache had become full-blown. Dexter grabbed the handle to pull the car door open for his parents. "Mother, I know you mean well, but I don't care a thing about Brittany. She doesn't appeal to me at all, and just because Dad is good friends with her father doesn't mean Brittany and I should end up as a couple. It's not going to happen." His voice had risen in volume with each sentence, and when he stopped speaking, both his parents had wide-eyed gazes. Yes, his message had come through loud and clear.

Dexter would never be disrespectful to his parents, and he normally didn't speak forcefully to them about any matter, but he'd had more than enough of their attempts to bring him and Brittany together. Not going to happen. Period.

~ ~ ~

Chapter 7

The next week seemed to pass in a blur. Claire had spoken privately to her boss, reminding him that moving was in her future—she just wasn't sure exactly when. To her relief, he'd understood and again told her a two-week notice would be sufficient, adding that she'd be missed in the office.

On Saturday, Claire met her uncle and cousin at her house in Peach Grove. The men planned to do minor repairs, and when they all arrived, the llamas were in the pasture. Claire had hoped to see them again and explained to her relatives about the neighbor she'd recently met. "I assured him I have no problem with his llamas grazing on my land. Besides, I think they're cute." She giggled, not missing her uncle's and cousin's amused expressions.

As they headed inside the house, her uncle explained the painter would begin after the electrical inspections had been done. It would be tempting to start bringing small items to her new home, but it was best to wait until all repairs, inspections, and the painting was completed.

She clutched the paint samples chart her uncle had brought and walked from room to room trying to imagine what color would look the best, excitement building inside her.

"This is a mighty big house for one person, Claire-Bear. But I imagine you won't stay single long, and the next thing we know, you'll be having young'uns." Her uncle grinned and Claire's cheeks warmed.

Uncle Ben meant well, so Claire didn't voice her thoughts to him. But the reality was that living on an acreage in Peach Grove meant being isolated—at least most of the time. Her choices wouldn't be plentiful in such a small, rural area. And given the fact she had no current romantic interest in her life, it appeared she'd need to adopt more cats.

To her aggravation, the image of Dexter popped into her mind. Why did she keep thinking about him? She hadn't even seen the man since the morning of her fender-bender. Sure, he'd been kind to make sure she was okay, but she didn't trust his motives. Maybe he was still hoping she'd change her mind about selling her property. After all, he'd sure been persistent in trying to buy it from her.

Her cousin's voice snapped her out of her musings. "How about we stop and eat at that diner when we leave here? I'll even treat." He grinned at her, reminding Claire of the mischievous boy he'd been when they were children. Back then he'd teased her, but he'd never been mean.

Claire laughed, insisting that she'd treat since he and his dad were doing the work for her. "We'll order a meal to-go for you to take Aunt Molly, since she couldn't join us today." Her aunt had been helping with a bridal shower at her church, otherwise she would've been there. Claire missed her, too. Even though she was perfectly at ease with her uncle and male cousin, it was always nice to have Molly in the group, sharing another woman's perspective on things.

"Yeah, your aunt hated missing out today, but she'd already committed to helping at church. I told Molly that the church would be lost without her helping to run things." Ben laughed, and his son nodded.

"It's great that Aunt Molly is so involved in activities. I'm hoping to find a good church here in Peach Grove after I move. I've been attending one in Fernwood, and it's nice, but I haven't taken part in anything extra there." A sense of longing unexpectedly filled Claire. She yearned to be in a community of down-to-earth folks who didn't put on airs. Fernwood had some nice, caring people. But there were also certain country club residents who seemed to think they were superior. Of course, not all the people who resided in the country club fit that description, but sadly, many of them did.

Yet again, her thoughts drifted to Dexter. Were he and his family some of the more affluent residents—the ones who regarded others as beneath them? Guilt poked at her. She shouldn't be thinking this way. True, many fit that mold, but it was wrong to automatically assume that Dexter and his parents fit that description. Still, she couldn't help wondering. Another reason he was so not her type, even if she was interested in him. Which, of course, she wasn't. Was she?

~ ~ ~

"Dexter, your father's having chest pains. An ambulance is on the way." His mother's trembling voice came through the phone on Monday morning, minutes before Dexter left his apartment to head to work.

"I'll be over right away, Mom. Try not to worry." Dexter's pulse raced as he rushed out to his car. He'd known his dad hadn't been feeling well the previous Friday, but hadn't thought it was anything serious. On the way to Brittany's party on Saturday, Carl had even commented about having heartburn. Now guilt poked him. He should've paid closer attention to his father's symptoms.

Often when Carl met an acquaintance for lunch at the country club, he'd later joke about eating too much, so Dexter had assumed that was the cause of his father's discomfort over the weekend. He sent up a brief prayer that his dad would be okay, which added to his guilt. He'd not been praying much in recent years, until now when he was feeling desperate.

He pulled up in front of his parents' stately home, noticing that the ambulance had already arrived. Good. The paramedics would tend to his father, and hopefully it wouldn't be anything major. Dexter's job would be to comfort and reassure his mother, which was a bit ironic, since he needed reassurance himself at the moment.

Taking a deep breath, he rushed into the house, relief filling him at his father's grumbling to everyone that he was fine. His mother appeared more in need of medical help than his father at that moment. She was pale, and her hands were shaking. Clearly, this had upset her greatly.

One of the paramedics spoke calmly but firmly. "Sir, we need to transport you to the hospital so the cardiologist on duty can assess your condition. It's likely that you're fine, as you said. But we'd prefer to play it safe." The man, who appeared to be in his forties, sent a smile to Dexter's mother and then to Dexter. Apparently, the paramedic had quickly figured out that Carl Jennings could be stubborn.

After assisting his mother into his car, Dexter drove behind the ambulance to the local hospital, which was only ten minutes away. He did his best to calm his mother, even joking about his dad's determination to convince everyone he was fine.

Two hours later, after some tests were run, color returned to his mother's face and relief washed over Dexter when the cardiologist informed them that his father should be fine. His discomfort had been due to severe indigestion—likely from his not-so-healthy diet and lack of exercise. Dexter had to suppress a laugh at seeing his father look sheepishly at the doctor and nod in agreement. Even Dexter's mother had now calmed down and was smiling at her husband's admissions that he must do better with his diet and exercise habits.

The doctor went on to talk about Carl's stress levels, asking questions about his job and his plans for the future. Dexter didn't miss the "I told you so" look his mother sent to her husband, especially when the doctor asked when Carl planned to retire.

After driving his parents back home, Dexter remained at their house for a while to make sure they were both okay. He insisted his father stay home that day, assuring him the real estate company could make it through a day without Carl Jennings in the office. Dexter also went over the diet and exercise regimen that had been sent home for his father to follow. Hopefully, this wake-up call would steer his father in a healthy direction. He wanted both his parents around for a long time.

Since Geneva had arrived, Dexter felt more at ease about leaving them, knowing the loyal housekeeper would make certain all was well. As he was about to head out the door, a florist delivery worker arrived with a large arrangement of cheery fall flowers. Dexter didn't have to see the card to know that Dora had sent them from the office, and he was glad he'd thought to let her know his father would be okay. The secretary had been more than a little worried when Dexter had phoned her from the hospital this morning.

Heading into the business district of Fernwood, Dexter glanced at his watch and realized it was past his usual lunchtime. After the stressful morning, he didn't have much of an appetite. Maybe he'd grab a salad at the pizza place and take it to the office. He phoned the secretary to tell her he was on the way. "How about letting me bring lunch to you?" Dexter enjoyed treating her now and then to show appreciation for her hard work.

To his surprise, she accepted his offer and admitted she'd love a slice of cheese pizza. Parking in the small lot of Skip's Pizzeria, Dexter hurried to the entrance of the small eatery, hoping he'd missed the lunch crowd. Two women were exiting at that moment, so Dexter stood back and held the door open for them. His pulse raced when he glanced at the taller one.

Claire and another woman were hurrying out, clutching their drinks and laughing. When she saw Dexter, her face lit up. Or maybe that was wishful thinking on his part. "Hello, Dexter. How are you?" She stood about two feet from him, but he caught a whiff of a fresh, floral scent. Definitely not from the Italian food in the pizzeria.

He smiled. "I'm tired. How are you?"

She responded saying she was fine, but wished it was Friday. Then she looked up at him again with a slight frown. "Are you feeling okay?"

He must look as exhausted as he felt. Dexter shook his head and briefly explained that his father had been rushed to the hospital but should be okay.

Genuine concern reflected in her blue eyes. "I'm so sorry, but I'm glad he'll be okay. That must have been scary for you and your family."

"Yeah, it was. It's just my parents and me, so I'm glad I could be there for my mom. She gets pretty shook up." He chuckled, trying to stay focused on their conversation rather than how pretty she looked. Her blonde hair hung below her shoulders, loose tendrils appearing even lighter against the burgundy dress she wore. Just then two more patrons exited the small building, so they needed to move.

Claire and her friend headed toward the parking lot, but she turned and spoke softly, "I'll be praying for your father. Have a nice weekend." She hesitated as though about to say more, but then turned and accompanied her friend toward the sidewalk. Dexter assumed they'd walked from their office building.

As he stepped to the counter to place his order, Dexter felt a sinking in his spirit. How he would've enjoyed chatting more with Claire, but what else could he say? Certainly, no questions about her property in Peach Grove. She'd likely think he was still hoping to purchase her land. Besides, her friend was with her, so that might've been awkward.

Still, while he waited for his food order to be filled, he couldn't help feeling he'd missed a chance to learn more about Claire. Maybe he should've stepped out of the doorway and at least tried to continue a conversation with her. Well, too late now. But as he drove to the real estate office, he wondered why on earth he was so drawn to a woman he knew so little about.

~ ~ ~

While making the short walk back to their office building, Claire smiled while Marcy chattered about the handsome man they'd just encountered. "You have to admit he's very good-looking. And he seems nice. Even though I wasn't part of the conversation, he glanced over at me and smiled."

Claire almost laughed at her friend sounding so pleased by a smile from Dexter. Yet she had to agree. He did seem more down-to-earth this time, but maybe that was due to his father's hospital trip that morning. "That's too bad his father was rushed to the hospital, but at least it wasn't a heart attack." They entered their office building, a gust of wind blowing behind them.

It occurred to her she'd not introduced Marcy and Dexter, so she apologized to her friend, who assured her it was no big deal.

"Since you weren't able to go with me this past Saturday, would you like to accompany me this next Saturday to my house?" Claire hadn't heard her friend mention another date with Tyler, her on-again-off-again boyfriend, and she didn't want to upset Marcy in case things weren't going well with him.

"Sure. I'd love that because Tyler is going on a fishing trip with his dad this weekend. How are the repairs coming?" Marcy's usual exuberance gave Claire a lift.

"My uncle's assured me that everything seems to be going well, so I should still be able to move in in late January or early February." Even as she spoke the words, Claire couldn't believe this was actually coming to fruition.

"I'd love to go with you. This isn't even my house, and I still get super excited." Marcy took another sip of her drink.

Claire smiled. "That's because you're such an amazing best friend. But don't let it go to your head." Both women laughed, then returned to their separate offices.

She shouldn't have been surprised that she had trouble keeping her mind on her work, and several times had to make corrections on some figures she'd entered. But to her annoyance, the image of Dexter kept appearing in her thoughts. Maybe she'd misjudged him. Maybe he had a caring heart. His actions the morning of her accident, and then spending half the day at the hospital with his parents were two examples that he must not be self-centered. A great catch for some woman. But not her. Claire didn't need to add a relationship to her crowded schedule at the moment. Now if she could only stop thinking about him.

~ ~ ~

When Dexter left his office on Friday afternoon, he

headed directly to his parents' home. The stone lions guarding the entrance to the Jennings' driveway always made him smile, and he'd secretly wanted to place golf caps on their heads—just to see his parents' reaction.

Dexter loved his parents, but had finally realized his goals in life were not the same as what they wanted for him. For years it had been assumed that Dexter would marry a woman from an upstanding family—preferably a family there in the Fernwood country club community—and continue working in his father's real estate business.

But the closer Dexter drew to age thirty, the more he questioned his own goals in life. Did he actually want what his parents wanted for him? The more he pondered that question, the more he realized the answer was no.

Heading to the side entrance of their home, Dexter shoved thoughts of his future from his mind. Right now, his priority was making sure his father was okay and his mother wasn't fretting too much. This medical scare had been hard on both of them. Not to mention the entire event had caused Dexter to do some serious soul-searching.

He entered his parents' house, greeted right away by the woodsy scent of pine cleaner. No doubt Geneva had recently cleaned the kitchen. He'd phoned to let his mother know he would be stopping by, and as footsteps approached, he wondered if she was coming to greet him. Instead, it was the housekeeper.

"Hello, Dexter. Your mother is resting at the

moment, but she wanted me to tell you that she'll be getting up in a few minutes. Your father is reading in his study. May I fix you something to drink?"

Ah, the usual formality of the Jennings household. A stranger observing the scene would think Dexter was a casual visitor, rather than the only son of the home's occupants.

He smiled and shook his head. "Thank you for the offer, but I'm fine, Geneva. Is it almost time for you to head home?" He hoped his mother wasn't expecting too much of the middle-aged employee, especially after his father's hospital incident.

She offered a smile and then shrugged. "I'm staying a bit later than usual today since your father has been ill. If you need something, please let me know. I'd better return to my ironing." She walked toward the spacious laundry room located not far from the kitchen.

Dexter headed in the direction of his father's study, wondering if he'd be asleep. Carl was awake and appeared relaxed. When he saw Dexter, the older man placed the book he'd been reading on his desk, then turned his full attention to his son.

"Hello, Dad. I thought you might be sleeping." Dexter was glad to see his father's coloring much improved from earlier in the week. That had been a scary experience, for certain.

Carl smiled and shook his head. "No, although I had a brief nap earlier today. How is the office? Any new developments? I'm trusting that Dora cancelled my

Friday appointments."

Dexter laughed and nodded, noticing his father was grinning. They never had to worry that Dora wouldn't handle things—competence seemed to be her middle name.

"Did you see the lovely flowers from the office? They were delivered on Monday and are still lovely." His father gestured in the direction of the kitchen.

"Yes, I'm glad they're on the kitchen table so you and Mom can enjoy them while you eat. They're beautiful. Everyone keeps asking about you and said to let you know they're concerned and want you to rest."

"I'm fine, and eager to get back to work." Even as Carl spoke, he became winded and began coughing.

Dexter cringed, but didn't say anything. His mother joined them. Had she heard his father's comment about getting back to work? He received the answer right away.

"Carl, dear. Aren't you overdoing it?" Her brow furrowed, but she quickly turned her attention to Dexter and patted his arm. "Hello, son. I hope you're planning to stay for supper. Did you see how fresh the beautiful flowers still are that the office sent?"

"Yes, the flowers are lovely, and if there's enough food, I'll stay and eat."

Obviously pleased with her son's response, his mother then focused her attention on Carl again. "You need to rest, and then afterward you can eat. Remember what the doctor told you." A hint of sharpness emphasized her words.

Dexter almost felt pity for his father at his mother's stern instructions, even though his mother spoke out of love for his dad. Trying to lighten the mood, he told his father they'd chat more after he rested, then Dexter followed his mother into the kitchen, where Geneva was setting the table.

Sitting at the table across from his mother, Dexter asked what he could do to help while his father recovered. He wasn't surprised at her reply.

"You can make sure he stops working so hard. Honestly, I'd thought for certain he would be retired by now. Completely retired. For years we've had so many plans to travel and enjoy life, but we can hardly do that with him putting in so many hours with the real estate business. I keep thinking that if you'd take over the company, he'll actually enjoy his retirement years."

There was no denying the resentment in his mother's comments about her husband retiring, and Dexter wasn't sure what to say. He nodded, then offered a feeble response, "Well, maybe before long Dad will officially retire, and you can take those trips." He stopped speaking before he said something that he'd regret.

It had been assumed for years that when the time came for Carl to retire, Dexter would take over the business. But he'd been having second thoughts—lots of second thoughts. Especially this past week as he ran the office in his father's absence. Is that what he wanted to do for the remainder of his working years? Recently he'd even wondered if he wanted to remain in Fernwood.

"This was a wake-up call for your father. I honestly believe that, son." The look she sent Dexter tugged at his heart. His mother wanted him to jump in and say he was ready to be completely in charge of the real estate company. But was he?

Dexter would not lie to his mother, so he simply reached across the table and patted her hand. "I'll talk with him, Mom. Things will work out, so please try not to worry. Just think about those trips you want to take and start planning." To his relief, his words had a calming effect on his mother. The remainder of his visit didn't include any talk about Dexter's future in the real estate company.

But as he returned to his apartment that evening, Dexter couldn't stop thinking about his mother's words and his own conflicting emotions. His parents expected him not only to continue in the real estate profession, but also offer leadership to the company his father had started decades earlier. The problem was that Dexter wasn't sure that's what he really wanted to do. But how could he disappoint his parents?

~ ~ ~

"They are adorable!" Marcy squealed at the sight of the llamas in the pasture. Claire pulled into the driveway of her Peach Grove house on Saturday morning, happy that her best friend had accompanied her.

"I told you they're cute. I'm so glad my neighbor

wants to continue using my pasture." She grinned and unbuckled her seat belt, eager to get busy inside the house. But first she and Marcy would head to the fence for a closer look at the llamas.

Two of the animals slowly ventured to the fence, as though making sure it was safe to approach the women. As Claire and Marcy spoke softly to them, the llamas came even closer, until they were within touching distance. "Do they bite?" Marcy glanced at Claire with widened eyes.

Claire shook her head. "The farmer assured me that unless they're provoked, they shouldn't bite." She slowly extended her hand to touch the fur between the llama's banana-shaped ears.

Marcy grinned and also stuck out her hand. "Okay, we're not provoking; we're just petting them." A giggle followed her words.

After about ten minutes, the women decided they'd better head inside the house and get busy, although they agreed it would be easy to remain at the fence, spending time with the llamas.

"Are you going to name them?" Marcy asked, as Claire unlocked the front door of the house.

Claire laughed. "I probably will, even though they're not really mine. They only use my pasture, but if I lived here all the time, I'd get attached to them, for sure." The women stepped into the empty house, their footfall echoing on the dusty floor.

After Claire locked the door behind them, she smiled

at Marcy. "It's just a habit, although I feel safe in this area."

Marcy eyed her thoughtfully, then moistened her lips before speaking, "Uh...I've been wanting to ask you something. Will you be okay living here?" When Claire frowned, Marcy continued. "You know—after what you went through in college. I just want to make sure you'll be okay living out here in the country, since..." Her voice trailed off, and her eyes held concern.

Reaching out and patting her friend's arm, Claire smiled. "Yes, and I know you've worried about me these past seven years, which means a lot. But I promise I'll be fine." As she noticed Marcy's skeptical look, she lightened the mood. "Besides, the llamas will guard me." She released a laugh and Marcy joined in, shaking her head.

After giggling and sharing silly comments about llamas dressed up as superheroes, the women got to work. Since Claire had brought basic cleaning supplies on her previous visit to the house, she opened the cabinet and lifted them out. "Are you sure you don't mind helping me with some cleaning? Uncle Ben said the repairs should begin next week, but it would be a good idea to do at least a little cleaning, so everything isn't super dirty by the time the repairs are finished."

Marcy grabbed some cloths and a spray bottle of cleaner, shaking her head. "Are you kidding? No, I don't mind helping you. This is exciting." She peered around at the large kitchen, then smiled at Claire. "I can't wait to see how you fix things up after you move in here. Have you decided on colors or a theme for your kitchen? Sunflowers? Fruit? Llamas?"

Both women erupted in laughter again. How blessed Claire was having Marcy in her life. Not only was her friend willing to pitch in and help her work in her house, but Marcy's enthusiasm was genuine.

An hour later, Claire headed out to her car to retrieve the small cooler she'd brought. The canned colas would offer a bit of refreshment for them, and she could tell Marcy needed a break. After grabbing the cooler, she closed her car door, then glanced out to the road when a car drove past. Would the farmer be stopping by while they were there?

The vehicle slowly driving past her property made her heart race. A small sports car with a single occupant inside inched by, and Claire had to make sure her mouth didn't drop open. If she wasn't mistaken—and she didn't think she was—the car belonged to Dexter Jennings. Although Claire hadn't gotten a good look at the driver, she felt certain it was him.

Why was he here in Peach Grove, driving slowly past her land? Was he still hoping she'd change her mind and sell her property? She'd made it clear to him that she was not selling. He wasn't some kind of stalker, or was he? The thought sent chills snaking up her spine. She needed to get a grip—minutes earlier she'd been laughing with Marcy, and now she was conjuring up a ridiculous notion about Dexter.

Claire hurried back inside the house, giving herself a mental chiding. The day she'd been hit in Fernwood, Dexter had remained near the scene of the accident to make certain she was okay. He seemed like a nice man, not some weirdo type. Maybe he was looking at other properties in the area. She decided not to mention seeing his car to Marcy because her friend would likely worry about her.

But for reasons she couldn't explain, Claire was more than a little curious as to why the handsome real estate agent had driven past her house. And she was aggravated with herself that she continued thinking about him so much.

~ ~ ~

On Saturday afternoon, Dexter drove back to Fernwood after a jaunt to Peach Grove. On a whim that morning, he'd decided to spend part of his day driving to the rural area and looking around. Who knows? Maybe he'd locate some other land that he and his father could develop.

Who are you kidding? You associate Peach Grove with Claire. Although he didn't actually expect to see her, he did. After driving around the tiny community, Dexter had turned around to return to Fernwood. As he'd driven past Claire's property, she was walking from her car toward the house, and she'd looked toward the road. He only hoped she didn't recognize his car because that might seem strange if she did.

He'd also seen some animals on her property, and Dexter had been tempted to pull into the driveway, yet he didn't dare. At first, he'd thought they were goats, but when he looked again, they appeared to be llamas. Did they belong to Claire? The llamas in her pasture added to the idyllic scene her property made. No wonder she didn't want to sell. Dexter almost cringed now at the thought of a subdivision—even a small one—being built on the pastoral land.

Surprisingly, the visit to Peach Grove had stirred his heart even more. What was going on with him? He'd always been a city dweller, preferring urban settings and offices. So why did a tiny, rural community appeal to him now? Was it simply due to the fact that he'd been unsuccessful at purchasing the property his father had wanted? After all, often when a person attempted to acquire something they couldn't have, it made them yearn all the more for it. But he didn't think that was it. No, something in that area itself beckoned him.

When he returned to his apartment, he phoned Howard. "Hey, are you still free to watch the game tonight? You can come over to my place if you are."

To Dexter's relief, Howard didn't have other plans, so he picked up a pizza and arrived at Dexter's around seven. The aroma of pepperoni and tomato wafted to Dexter's nose as his friend entered the apartment.

"Thanks for getting that. I'll pay you." Dexter reached for his wallet, but Howard insisted it was his treat, since Dexter often paid for their food.

Although he'd not planned on opening up to Howard, Dexter ended up telling his friend about his drive to Peach Grove that day. During commercials he'd add a few more details, omitting the part about seeing Claire on her property.

"There's just something about that area. Which is strange for me because I've always figured I'd remain in a city my entire life." He didn't miss the amused look Howard was giving him.

Before biting into another slice of pizza, Howard nodded. "Yeah, this is surprising, man. I'd always thought you'd stay in Fernwood forever. Or if not Fernwood, then maybe a bigger city. But definitely a city, not out in the country." Howard shook his head as though puzzled.

"What's had me worried is my dad's work situation. Now that he's had that health scare, my mom is really on him about retiring. And of course, they assume I'll take over the real estate company and carry on." Dexter stopped talking when the commercial ended, and the football game resumed.

But during the next commercial, Howard studied him with curious eyes. "I don't get it. Are you saying you don't want to remain in your father's real estate company?"

Dexter didn't answer right away, but slowly reached for another pizza slice. Then he shrugged. "I'm not sure. Up until recently, I'd thought my future plans were set.

I'd keep working in the company, and maybe one day get married and have a family, then settle in a house here in Fernwood. Now I'm not so sure anymore." He bit into the pizza and chewed thoughtfully, noting the puzzlement on Howard's face.

For the remainder of the evening, the football game took precedence, and all conversation centered around sports. But after Howard left the apartment, Dexter couldn't stop thinking of what he'd shared with his friend. He'd not planned on saying anything, yet his thoughts had slipped out. Was he just going through some weird phase—thinking he wanted a different lifestyle?

He planned on spending the following day with his parents. Dexter had already told his mother that he'd pick up a meal from the Fernwood Bistro since Geneva was off on Sundays. Would his mother bring up his dad's retiring and Dexter taking over the business? He sincerely hoped not. Until he'd thought more about his future plans, he certainly didn't want to mention anything to his parents.

But he couldn't deny that the idea of doing something other than going to an office in Fernwood each day appealed to him. The problem was Dexter had no idea what he could do. Not to mention the minor detail of where he'd live, if not in Fernwood.

Underneath his whirling thoughts, the image of a certain blonde-haired woman kept appearing in his mind, which only added to his confusion. Did a life in a rural setting appeal to him because he associated it with Claire? The very idea was preposterous. He'd never been one to act on impulse, yet now he was doing it more and more.

Although Dexter had pulled away from a close relationship with God in recent years, it might be a wise decision to pray and read his Bible for guidance, rather than trusting his own thoughts. With his current confused state, it had to help.

~ ~ ~

Mid-November brought chilly temperatures and more colorful leaves. Claire hurried into the logistics office on Monday morning, breathing in the crisp autumn air. She grinned at the receptionist, who was placing an adorable set of Thanksgiving decorations on one area of the counter.

"It's hard to believe it's that time of year again." Claire signed in, then looked at the woman.

"I know. And before we can blink, it'll be Christmas. Are you ready?" The receptionist giggled, adding another tiny pilgrim to the holiday display.

"No, although I do love the holidays. This year has gone too fast for me. How are you feeling?" She gestured toward the woman's growing midsection. The receptionist had glowed since announcing her pregnancy. Claire fought the underlying envy that niggled at her, wondering if she'd ever experience that for herself.

The receptionist beamed. "Now that the nausea is about gone, I'm doing much better. Thanks for asking. I keep thinking that this time next year, my holidays will be vastly different." She lovingly placed a hand on her middle.

Claire smiled and turned to head to her small office room. "Your holidays will be extra exciting, for sure." She was genuinely happy for her, especially since the woman was almost forty and didn't think she'd ever have a child.

The aroma of fresh-brewed coffee prompted Claire to deposit her handbag and jacket in her office, then scurry down the hall to the breakroom to grab a cup of the warm liquid. Although she always drank a cup at home in the mornings, she was thankful her company provided unlimited coffee to their employees.

"How is it Monday again?" Marcy sleepily trudged into the breakroom, her groggy appearance causing Claire to wonder if her friend was ill.

"Yeah, the weekends go fast. Are you okay? How was your Sunday with your relatives?" Claire had missed seeing her at church and hanging out the previous day, but had used her afternoon to pack in preparation for her upcoming move, even though it was still two months away.

"It was fine. I always enjoy seeing my relatives—especially my cousins. But whenever we have one of our large gatherings, I always eat way too much. Then I stayed up too late going through old photos one of my cousins had given me."

"Sounds fun. You're blessed to have such a large family." Claire smiled, again fighting a twinge of envy. What was wrong with her today? Envious of the pregnant receptionist and now envious of her best friend's abundance of relatives. *Count your blessings.* The silent reminder drifted through her thoughts.

Marcy looked remorseful. "Oh, I know I am, and they're wonderful. It's just that these mini-reunions wear me out, not to mention the fact that several well-meaning aunts and uncles keep dropping hints about me having a wedding. They've forgotten that for me to have a wedding, I'll need a groom." Marcy laughed, then reached for the coffee pot to fill her large mug.

"Yeah, a little minor detail." Claire took a sip of her coffee and headed toward the door. She needed to get started on her projects for the week because if she did, in fact, leave this company within the next few months, she wanted to be ahead on her workload and not leave her replacement at a disadvantage.

Marcy stopped her with a question. "Speaking of grooms, have you seen Dexter recently?"

That pesky blush crept up Claire's face—she could feel it. "No, and why on earth would you associate Dexter with a groom?" Was she that transparent? Did her friend know how many of Claire's thoughts centered around the handsome real estate agent? Nah, that was impossible. Marcy knew her well, but no one could read another person's mind, could they?

Marcy now eyed Claire with an impish grin. "Well, for starters, he's incredibly good-looking, and doesn't every bride hope for a good-looking groom?" She winked at Claire.

Shaking her head, Claire released a playful groan and headed to her office. Definitely time to get to work. She needed to shove thoughts of Dexter far from her mind and focus on her job. Yet it was interesting that her friend seemed to discern Claire's secret fascination with the real estate agent. Okay, maybe *fascination* was too strong of a word. But there was no denying that Dexter Jennings had gotten under her skin and was somehow getting under her heart, too.

~ ~ ~

Carl Jennings phoned Dexter on Monday afternoon, asking his son to stop by on his way home. It was no secret his father was disgruntled that he couldn't return to the office yet, per his doctor's orders. In the meantime, Dexter's mother was doing her best to convince Carl that he needed to retire—completely.

Dexter was torn, not sure what to do regarding his future. The fact he didn't have a plan only added to his frustration. All he knew was that he wanted—no, *needed*—a change. But he didn't want to let his father down.

After picking up salads and fruit at Fernwood's

upscale deli, Dexter arrived at his parents' home, relieved that their housekeeper had already gone home. He worried that his mom sometimes overworked Geneva, although he'd never verbalize those concerns to his mother.

"Hello, dear." His mother greeted him in the kitchen, obviously pleased with the food he'd picked up. "Thank you for bringing our supper meal. After you phoned from your office and mentioned it, I told Geneva to go on home."

"I'm glad to bring food—although it's certainly nothing fancy. Geneva seems to work hard, so that's good she went home." He clamped his lips together, not wanting to stir up anything.

Carl joined them at the kitchen table, his color looking even better now after resting for a few more days. The conversation was pleasant—general comments about the weather and traffic in Fernwood. But just as Dexter had expected, the conversation took a major turn as they finished their meal.

"Son, this health episode, as your mother calls it, has been a wake-up call for me. I suppose it's time I retire. Not a part-time situation, but a full retirement. I've given this a lot of thought and have decided that your mother is right." Carl paused and offered a weak smile in his wife's direction. She beamed and patted his hand. "Anyway, as soon as my doctor gives me the all-clear, I'll return to the office long enough to wrap things up and turn the business over to the new leader."

Dexter's heart pounded so strongly that he hoped his parents didn't hear it. He swallowed, feeling as though every bite of his salad and pecan pie were now caught in his throat. Remaining silent, he stared at his father with a neutral expression, waiting to see what he would say next.

In a softer voice, the older man asked the question that Dexter knew was inevitable. "Are you interested in taking over the company?" Before Dexter could respond, his father held up a hand and continued, "I've always assumed that when the time came for me to retire, you'd step right in and head the company. But..." His voice trailed off, and he cast a swift glance in his wife's direction, then refocused on Dexter. "If that's not what you want, I'd never want to force you to take over." His tone and the softened gaze in his father's gray eyes let Dexter know he was sincere.

His mother nodded, sending a gentle smile to her son.

For a few moments, silence hung in the air, so thick it could be sliced just as the pecan pie had been minutes earlier. Dexter's hands felt shaky, which was silly. These were his parents, after all. It wasn't as though he was meeting with people he barely knew. Still, this was a conversation he'd rather not have, but knew he must.

Forcing a smile, Dexter glanced at his mother, then focused on his father. "I'm glad you'll be retiring, Dad. Most of all, for your health, but also so you and Mom can enjoy life. I know Mom wants to travel, and you should." He paused, almost wishing he had words prepared on a note card, so he could simply read his reply to his parents. But that was absurd.

He cleared his throat. "I'm having some, um…thoughts about my future. Trying to decide what I really want to do." Well, this wasn't coming out as he'd like, and the looks his parents were giving him made him feel ridiculous. Maybe he should just stop talking and tell his father he'd think about things and talk with him later.

Surprisingly, his father nodded and stroked his chin. "Okay, son. You decide what you honestly want to do and let me know. As much as I love the company, I'd never want you to take over if your heart wasn't in it." A flicker of sadness passed over his face, but then he smiled. "One thing this health scare has shown me is that life is fragile. And short. Being happy is not overrated, so you want to plan your future accordingly."

Dexter was stunned. His father wasn't normally so philosophical, but his comments touched Dexter's heart. He nodded and thanked him, then turned his attention to his mother, who'd remained unusually quiet while listening to the conversation.

"So, Mom, tell me about some of the trips you have planned for Dad's retirement years." He hoped the abrupt change of topic wasn't too obvious, but to Dexter's relief, his mother began chattering about cities in Europe she'd love to visit.

Thirty minutes later, Dexter drove to his apartment. His mind replayed his father's words about life being short. He supposed this recent health scare had actually changed Carl in some ways, and Dexter had to admit that he was surprised. Although he hated that his father had experienced digestive issues, at least it encouraged Carl to make retirement plans and not keep putting it off.

Hopefully, his father's health would improve so he and Dexter's mom could travel. They deserved to enjoy their retirement years. But now the big question hovering in Dexter's mind was what to do about his own future. And it was a decision he'd never thought would be so difficult.

~ ~ ~

Chapter 8

Claire glanced at the calendar in her small office. How could November be going so quickly? Thanksgiving would be here before she knew it, which meant another opportunity to be with her relatives. That gave her heart a lift, and at this point she needed one. Recently she'd been feeling a bit overwhelmed with all she had to do before relocating to Peach Grove.

What drained her the most was the worry. Claire had been certain she was making the right decision to move to the tiny community and live in her inherited house. But lately doubts had crept in, and they were getting stronger.

She needed to talk with Marcy, but not here at work. No, they needed a girls' day together, so they had plenty of time to visit and share a meal. Maybe even do a little shopping. Yet now that Marcy was dating Tyler again, she'd been busier and not always as available as she'd been in the past. Claire was happy for her but still needed her best friend.

At lunchtime, she stuck her head into Marcy's office to see what she was doing for lunch. Her friend wore a silly grin and was just putting away her phone. She looked up as Claire tapped at the doorway.

"Hey there. I'm about to grab my sandwich and head to the breakroom. Want to join me? Tyler just texted to see if I want to go out to eat this Friday evening." That explained the grin on her face.

Claire smiled. "Sure. I set my tuna salad in the breakroom refrigerator, so I'll be eating that today, although I could really go for a pizza one day this week."

Marcy joined her and they headed toward the breakroom. Marcy's brows furrowed at Claire's face. "Hey, are you okay? You look like something is bothering you." They stepped into the room, occupied only by two other workers who were reading as they ate.

In a lowered voice, Claire told Marcy she'd been worried about her moving plans. "Any chance you'd be free on Saturday? You said you have a date Friday evening, so if you also have plans on Saturday, it's okay." Claire hoped she didn't sound as frustrated as she was feeling.

Marcy patted her arm. "Yes, I'm free on Saturday. Plus, then I can tell you about my exciting time with Tyler on Friday." She laughed, the sound boosting Claire's mood a bit.

The remainder of their lunchtime was spent chatting about their current work projects and how fast the year was passing by. Forty-five minutes later the friends returned to their respective offices, and Claire found herself looking forward to spending time with Marcy on Saturday. Now, if she could stay focused on her work and finish the assignments she had to complete before the end of the year. Because when she did finally move to Peach Grove, Claire wanted to be sure that she'd finished all her commitments to her employer.

Now the big question hovering in her mind was about employment. What would she do for work after she moved to Peach Grove? She was blessed to have a substantial amount from her late mother's insurance, but she couldn't live on that forever. Claire had a lot of praying to do.

~ ~ ~

Dexter was thankful his father's health was improving. Carl was getting stronger by the day, according to Dexter's mother. He'd even planned to reduce his time at the real estate office, stopping in only to begin the process of handing the reins over. The big question remained—who would take over the business?

From various comments the other employees made, they all assumed that as Carl's son, Dexter would be the one to take over the business. No one at the real estate company had a clue that he was even considering leaving the business. Not only that, but also leaving the area. Of course, he'd make absolutely certain his father's health was good before doing that. But the way his mother was already planning their future travels, Dexter had a strong feeling his dad was definitely on the mend.

Going about his routine duties of following up on

clients and checking on the employees at the company, Dexter realized more and more that he needed a change. He couldn't imagine spending his remaining working years in Fernwood at the company his father had started. And that caused guilt to poke at him on a daily basis. Yet hadn't his father himself told Dexter that life was short, and he needed to be happy in his career?

His ringing cell phone startled him, and he grabbed it. His father's voice came through, sounding like his old self. "Hey son, are you still in the office?"

"Hi, dad. Just about to leave. What do you need? Do you and Mom want me to bring supper for you?"

His father chuckled good-naturedly, sending Dexter's curiosity level soaring. Although he laughed now and then, as a rule, Carl Jennings wasn't considered a jovial type.

"No, but thank you for offering. Geneva cooked a big pot of beef stew that should last us for several meals. You're welcome to join us. But what I phoned about was an interesting conversation I had today with Neal Sims. Would you have time to stop by on your way home?"

After assuring his father he'd be at their house shortly, Dexter headed out, wondering about this conversation that had his father in a chipper mood. When Dexter entered his parents' home, the aroma of beef stew greeted him, reminding him of how hungry he was. Maybe he would join his parents for supper if there was enough.

His mother welcomed him, gesturing to the large pot

simmering on the stove. "Please eat with us. Even if your father and I have leftovers three times, this is still too much. Bless Geneva, she tends to go overboard with her cooking. But I'm not complaining." She lifted the lid and stirred the stew.

Dexter resisted the urge to tell his mother he was glad she wasn't complaining, because Geneva had been a jewel for his parents. Not only hardworking and dependable, but an excellent cook, as well.

Carl joined them and minutes later the three adults sat at the kitchen table, enjoying the savory stew, cornbread, and fruit salad that Geneva had prepared. Although eager to hear about his father's conversation with Neal Sims, Dexter decided to let his father broach the subject first.

"Everyone at the office sends their best wishes, and they're all glad you're doing so much better." Dexter didn't miss the look of pride in his father's eyes. His dad had worked hard to build a successful company, including earning the respect of his employees.

As he finished his bowl of stew, Carl peered at his son. "I told you Neal Sims phoned me today, and we had a nice conversation. He wanted to check on my health, and then we talked about his recent golf games. It was good to hear from him."

Even though Neal was a good bit younger than his dad, the two men had hit it off and often played golf together and shared lunches at the country club in recent years. But something in his father's expression told him this was about more than golf scores.

Carl cleared his throat, took a sip of his iced tea, and continued. "Anyway, Neal knows I've planned to retire for quite some time. He assumed—correctly, of course—that with my recent health scare, my retirement would be sooner rather than later." Another pause, then he got right to the point. "He's interested in buying my company."

Wow. Dexter caught a glimpse of his mother's look of shock. Had she not known about this? Then he realized her shock was the manner in which his father had broken the news to him. But then, his father usually preferred to get directly to the heart of a matter.

Silence hung in the air, as though his parents were waiting to hear his reaction. Had he heard his father correctly? His friend wanted to buy the real estate company? Dexter's mind whirled, trying to absorb what this meant. Yet underneath was the realization that Dexter wouldn't have to feel guilty for not taking over the business.

A breath whooshed out of him. His parents' faces held curiosity, and a bit of amusement. Apparently, this wasn't the reaction they'd expected. Dexter smiled and met both their gazes.

"Wow. That's big news, Dad. How would you feel about a friend running the real estate business?"

A slow smile spread across his father's face. "If you'd asked me that question before my health scare, I'd have been emphatic in saying no way. But now…I realize how special each day is, so if you decide to head in another direction, I'm good with Neal taking over." Dexter had never heard him speak in this manner. Especially the comment about each day being special.

Dexter smiled and nodded. "That's awesome. You've worked so hard for so long, and you deserve to feel good about what happens to the company you've built." He didn't miss the look of relief that passed over his father's face.

His mother quickly changed the topic, excitedly describing the travels she planned on the couple taking. "As soon as your father is strong enough, because I certainly don't want him to feel weak while we're traveling. I want him to enjoy every minute." She sent a loving smile to her husband.

When Dexter drove to his apartment thirty minutes later, he replayed their conversation in his mind. He'd never observed his parents so heartfelt in their mealtime talks. It must be due to his father's health, which had given them both a scare, and now they were thankful he was doing much better.

Unlocking his apartment door, Dexter felt as though a weight had been lifted off him. If his father was genuinely at peace with a friend purchasing and taking over the real estate business, that freed up Dexter to pursue his own interests. Even if that meant moving out of Fernwood.

Yet the obvious questions remained. Where would he go, and what type of work would he do? Abruptly, the peaceful feeling from seconds earlier evaporated. Dexter had some larger-than-life decisions to make.

~ ~ ~

"I don't guess the holidays are the best time to make serious decisions about your future." Dexter spoke the words with a hint of dry humor as he grabbed more French fries. He had picked up burgers and fries for Howard and himself, and now they sat in Dexter's small apartment kitchen.

Howard shrugged. "Actually, since this is a happy time of year, it might be a good time to analyze what you want out of life." He bit into his burger.

Dexter suppressed a laugh at his friend's philosophical comment. But the more he thought about it, the more he decided Howard might be right. Besides, it wasn't as though his schedule was filled with holiday parties to attend or a large amount of shopping. He planned to purchase Christmas gifts for his parents, of course, and get something for Howard. *No female to shop for this year.* He ignored the thought.

Howard left Dexter's apartment a few hours later, after the friends had viewed two football games on television. Right before leaving, Howard had mentioned going to church the next morning, sending a niggle of guilt through Dexter. He'd not been to church in quite a while, but he had his reasons. Mostly, the fact that he still wasn't on the best terms with God at the moment. He'd feel like a hypocrite walking into the worship service at Fernwood Christian Church, although his parents usually attended there and would be glad to see him show up.

The guilt didn't disappear because the next morning Dexter stumbled out of bed in time to get dressed for the eleven o'clock worship service. He planned to sit near the back and hurry out as soon as the service ended.

When he arrived at the church doors about ten minutes before eleven, two men greeted people as they entered the building. One of the men was Neal, his father's friend. Recognition dawned in the middle-aged man's eyes. "Good to see you, and I'm so thankful Carl is feeling much better now. He gave us all a scare."

Dexter smiled. "Yes, we're all happy that he's doing much better now. My mother is especially glad he's finally ready to retire so they can travel." He was eager to find a vacant spot on the last pew in the worship building, but the church was filling fast.

Neal leaned forward. "If you wouldn't mind sticking around a few minutes when the service ends, I'd like to talk with you. It won't take long." He grinned, as though assuring Dexter he'd be brief.

"Sure, no problem." Dexter nodded again, then hurried to claim a seat. He gazed around the large room, but didn't see his parents. The lovely music soothed him. He was actually glad he'd decided to attend church—maybe it would become a habit again. He attempted to shove away thoughts of Neal wanting to speak with him. Likely it was connected to purchasing and taking over his father's real estate company, which Dexter had no qualms about the man doing.

Dexter enjoyed the whole service—more than he'd thought he would. The pastor's sermon was uplifting and easy to follow, and the choir sang a medley of old familiar hymns that Dexter liked. Hopefully, Neal wouldn't talk long so Dexter could head home when the pastor finished the closing prayer.

His father's friend was waiting outside the church doors, so Dexter joined him, and they eased away from the others who were still exiting the service. Dexter was a tiny bit nervous, which was ridiculous. There was no reason to be nervous around Neal.

After a couple of comments about the pastor's uplifting sermon, Neal got right to the point. "As I'm sure you know, I've spoken with Carl about purchasing the real estate company. He was agreeable, and said he was quite certain you didn't want to take over when your father retires." Neal paused and drew in a deep breath. "I just want to make absolutely certain I'm not stepping on your toes, so to speak. If you've changed your mind, just let me know."

A sigh of relief almost escaped from Dexter's mouth, but he suppressed it. Instead, he smiled at Neal and shook his head. "I haven't changed my mind, but I do appreciate this. When Dad told me you're interested, I was relieved." He paused, choosing his words carefully. "In recent months, I've been having second thoughts about taking over the business, and finally decided that's not what I really want to do. Dad has been supportive—especially since his health scare."

Neal's face registered compassion, as though he understood Dexter's struggle to do the right thing. "Yes, sometimes a wake-up call reminds us of what is truly important in life. Your father has worked hard for decades, so he and your mother deserve to enjoy their retirement years. I still have a good dozen years to go before retirement, but I want to make the most of them."

Dexter nodded, filled with an assurance that Neal would be the one to take over his father's company. Now if he could only figure out what *his* future plans should be, he'd feel even better.

~ ~ ~

Claire's uncle phoned her with an update the Saturday before Thanksgiving, assuring her that the small team of repairmen he'd recruited were on schedule, even though they could only work certain weekends. "No worries, Claire-Bear. That's a blessing of living in Georgia—our fall and winter seasons rarely have extreme weather. If you still want to make plans to move into your house in late January, that should work. Now here's your aunt, chomping at the bit to speak to you."

Her uncle's comments reassured her, but her aunt's giggles brought a smile to her face. Aunt Molly interrupted. "Your uncle just compared me to a horse.

But that's okay—horses are beautiful. You might even decide to have some horses on your property someday."

"Hey, Aunt Molly. Yes, horses are beautiful creatures, so maybe I'll take your suggestion someday. How are you doing?"

"I'm busy as a bumblebee, but thankful my health is holding up, overall. Just the usual aches and pains that come with getting older." She chuckled, then chatted about the family's upcoming Thanksgiving dinner, insisting that Claire join them. "And you don't need to bring a thing, even though you always do. But really, dear, there's no need. We'll have plenty of food."

A warmth spread through Claire at her aunt's comments. How thankful she was to have relatives who truly loved her and included her in activities—especially since her own parents were gone, and she had no siblings.

After chatting for ten more minutes, the call ended. Claire glanced out one of the few windows in her small apartment, noting the blustery day. She was glad to have supper plans with Marcy. She was also glad they'd decided to order pizza and eat at Marcy's apartment. Claire needed to treasure these frequent visits with her friend because after she moved to Peach Grove, it would be more difficult to get together.

That thought sent a wave of emotion through Claire—sadness, accompanied by a bit of fear. She was being silly because it wasn't as though she and Marcy would never see each other. Their visits in person just wouldn't happen quite as often. Besides, Marcy had told her to think of this as an adventure in her life. Yes, it would be an adventure, all right. Relocating from an upscale city to a tiny rural community should prove to be adventurous.

On a whim, Claire opened up her laptop and went to a link she'd saved about llamas. She'd read a little about them after meeting her farmer neighbor, but now she had a desire to learn all she could about the animals. At least thinking of the cute critters who grazed on her land kept the melancholic feelings at bay.

At six o'clock, Marcy arrived, grinning like the Cheshire Cat. At first Claire assumed her friend was looking forward to the pizza, but she soon learned the true reason for the wide smile. She bustled into Claire's apartment and plopped onto the sofa. "Guess who phoned me this afternoon?"

Before Claire could answer, Marcy was babbling about Tyler calling and asking her to eat with him after church the next day. "It's crazy for me to be this excited about a simple phone call because it was so casual. But the fact he wants us to go out tomorrow afternoon gives me hope that maybe he regrets breaking up with me a while back." A happy glow lit up her face, so Claire chose to express enthusiasm but also added a word of caution, not wanting Marcy to get hurt again.

"That is great! Just please be careful, Marcy. Don't let him think you're too eager to resume dating again because he won't appreciate you as much." She offered a sympathetic smile that turned into a giggle. "Yeah, listen to me giving dating advice. What a joke. I'm not exactly fighting off the guys myself, but that's okay. Guess it's a blessing I'm not dating anyone at the moment because it would make this move to Peach Grove even harder."

Marcy reached over and patted her hand. "That's the way to keep a good attitude. And you never know—the man of your dreams might appear in Peach Grove."

Raising a skeptical eyebrow, Claire grinned. "A little far-fetched, but I appreciate your positive thinking. Now, let's eat."

As the friends finished their meal, Marcy sent a hesitant gaze to Claire. "I hate to ask this, because you have plenty to think about right now, but have you decided what to do about a job after you move?"

Claire released a sigh and shook her head. "No, and I'll have to decide something, since my insurance money won't last forever." She didn't miss the concern in Marcy's eyes and knew her friend was worried about her. To lighten the conversation, Claire shrugged. "Maybe I could be a server at Retha's Diner, except I'd be dropping everyone's meals and drinks. Can you imagine?"

Both women laughed at the image Claire described, agreeing that would not be the ideal job for her. Before Claire could comment further, Marcy piped up, her usual enthusiasm coming through.

"Remember a while back when I suggested you do

something with your photography? You really have talent, Claire, and just think of the pictures you can take when you're living in the country." Marcy's gaze took on a faraway look, as though imagining different scenes in the picturesque community.

Claire nodded, a tiny surge of excitement building at her friend's suggestion. After all, she had received many compliments in recent years for photos she'd taken and had even framed some to give as gifts.

Marcy continued, her eyes widening as she spoke. "Remember that sunflower field we passed up the road from your land? There was a sign advertising the sunflowers, and when they're in full bloom, I'm sure they're gorgeous."

"You're right. A large field of sunflowers in bloom would make a great photo." Claire nodded, thinking her friend's suggestion might be worth seriously considering. Although selling her photography wouldn't make enough to live on, it would certainly help.

Later that night after Marcy went home, Claire poured some dry cat food into her felines' bowls and thought about the plans she and Marcy had discussed. Claire's move was looming closer. The holidays were almost upon them, and then before she knew it, she'd be headed to the tiny community almost two hours away.

She'd be all alone—well, except for her cats. And the llamas. At the thought of the cute animals who grazed on her land, she smiled. A friend had called her a crazy cat lady as a joke. Would she soon be labeled a crazy llama lady?

~ ~ ~

Thanksgiving arrived along with chilly weather. Fernwood had its usual autumn décor displayed throughout the community, and Dexter had often wondered just how much the city spent on the upscale seasonal decorations. Sure, it was nice touch, but in his opinion, the Fernwood garden club went a bit overboard, as though they were trying to outdo any surrounding communities.

Dexter's parents had paid Geneva a bonus to prepare Thanksgiving dinner, allowing enough to take home for her own family. When Dexter arrived mid-day, clutching a pie and flowers for his mother, the aromas from the meal greeted him at the door. Geneva was an excellent cook, so he was certain this meal would be wonderful.

"Come in, Dexter. Geneva just left to take food home and enjoy the remainder of the day with her family. Some families request that their maids work on holidays, but that doesn't seem right to me." His mother placed a well-manicured hand near her neck, as though the very idea appalled her. Dexter could only imagine some of the friends to whom his mother referred. Fernwood had some kind, caring residents, but also had its share of those who tended to think their wealth placed them above others.

"I thought about inviting Brittany to join us, but your

father didn't think I should." Eve turned away quickly, as though avoiding eye contact with her son.

"Why on earth would you do that?" Dexter didn't want to sound disrespectful to his mother, but the idea she'd even consider that sent his blood pressure soaring.

At that moment, Carl sauntered into the kitchen to join them, apparently hearing enough of their talking to know why his son's voice had risen in volume. He shook his head and patted Dexter on the shoulder. "Happy Thanksgiving, son. And no worries. Your mother had good intentions, but I thought you'd want to enjoy this day with only our family." His father winked at him, seeming to understand that Dexter had zero interest in the woman. Finally. Now if his mother could only be convinced of that fact.

Much to Dexter's relief, the conversation switched gears to the delectable meal Geneva had prepared, then to his mother's travel plans once his father's retirement was official. Dexter almost choked on his iced tea when his father casually commented that he didn't want a lot of fanfare made over him when he retired. It was no secret his father enjoyed being in the spotlight. In fact, the company secretary had already made plans for a special retirement reception.

After spending the remainder of Thanksgiving Day at his parents' home, which included watching football on television and eating more pie, Dexter hugged them and started out the door to his car. His mother grabbed his jacket sleeve to stop him. He swung around to see her looking at him with an expression of remorse.

She leaned closer to him, and in a soft tone apologized. "I shouldn't have even considered inviting Brittany today, dear, and I'm sorry that upset you. I-I just keep hoping you'll find someone to settle down with. I don't want to see you grow old alone." She lowered her eyes, then met his gaze again. This was a rare moment for his mother who was usually so assertive.

Dexter stepped back inside the back door and hugged her. "It's no big deal, Mom. You meant well. It's just that Brittany is not my type. And I have a few years before I'll be sent out to pasture." He chuckled, glad to see his mother smiling up at him.

Returning to his apartment, Dexter was more aware of the emptiness there. Sure, he had nice furnishings and even a few paintings hung on the walls. But it was only him. Strangely, he'd never felt this alone before, and he attributed that feeling to his mother's concerned comment. He would enjoy having a special someone in his life, but definitely *not* one of the Fernwood Country Club bachelorettes. No matter how upstanding or wealthy their families were, those women didn't hold any appeal for Dexter.

To his surprise, his mind filled with an image of Claire Durham. He'd not even seen her recently, and for all he knew, she might have a beau. But for reasons he didn't want to analyze, he couldn't stop thinking about her, and that puzzled him.

~ ~ ~

Chapter 9

For the very first time since living on her own, Claire didn't put up her small Christmas tree. She was tempted, but knew the more items she could pack, the easier her upcoming move would be. At least she had some small items she could display to help keep her in the Christmas spirit, including her small Nativity scene and a few snowmen figurines. When she'd lamented the lack of a tree this year, Marcy had reminded her that next Christmas she'd be decorating her lovely country home.

The first week of December arrived with a chill in the air, along with lavish Christmas decorations throughout Fernwood. Claire wondered if Peach Grove had many Christmas activities—after all, it was such a small community.

Saturday evening, Claire talked with her aunt, again thanking her for the wonderful Thanksgiving meal the previous week. After clicking off her cell phone, a warmth flooded her. How blessed she was to have a wonderful aunt and uncle like hers. Molly reminded Claire to join their family for Christmas, insisting the holiday wouldn't be complete without her.

Molly had even teased her, suggesting that maybe next Christmas Claire would be hosting a family gathering in her country home. Claire had laughed and agreed, then the women began discussing plans for their Christmas dinner.

Now as Claire folded her basket of laundry, she imagined what her Peach Grove house might look like next year. Excitement surged through her at the possibilities. An entire house to decorate—just as she'd like. Garlands on the banisters, greenery and candles on the mantel, her list went on and on. She could barely fall asleep because her mind whirled with decorating ideas.

The next morning, she groggily dressed for church. Although Claire enjoyed attending church year-round, the Christmas season was extra special. Beautiful wreaths decorated the doors, and poinsettias circled the podium where the preacher stood. Even the church windows held greenery and candles, and the Christmas music always filled Claire with a sense of peace.

Marcy texted just as Claire pulled into the church parking lot. She'd awakened with a sore throat, so was staying home that day. After Claire had turned off her engine and then read the message, she sent a quick reply telling her friend to rest. A tiny bit of apprehension ran through Claire, which was silly. She'd sat alone before at church, so it shouldn't be a big deal.

After accepting a bulletin from the middle-aged gentleman who greeted her at the door, Claire hurried inside the worship building to find a seat near the back. Whew! There was some space on the next to last row, so she slipped in and sat down just as the music began. Her mind drifted to what the Peach Grove church might be like. Would the people be friendly? If the congregation was anything like the customers in Retha's Diner, the answer would be a resounding yes.

She snapped her mind back to the service when the pastor began his usual meaningful sermon. Time passed quickly, and before she knew it, the service ended. Claire gathered her handbag and stuck the bulletin inside, then made her way toward the door to leave. As usual, some familiar faces smiled at her and wished her a merry Christmas, which she appreciated.

Just as she stepped outside, a male voice called to her. "Claire?" A tingle ran through her. She knew that voice. Slowly turning around, she saw Dexter coming toward her, a smile on his handsome face. The suit he wore only emphasized his good looks, and Claire fought the nervousness filling her.

"Hello. I didn't see you in the service." Not that she'd been looking, but what else could she say?

"I sat with my parents on the right side, but saw you heading toward the door. Are you all ready for Christmas?"

"Yes, pretty much. I'll still buy some small items for relatives and my friend, Marcy, but shopping's done for the most part. Which is a good thing since I've got a lot to do before my move." Why on earth had she babbled on and mentioned her move?

His eyebrows furrowed at her comment, and he leaned in a bit closer. The scent of his musky cologne reached Claire's nose, and for some reason she had the crazy urge to ask him the name of it. Thankfully, she didn't.

"You're moving for sure? To the house on your land in Peach Grove?" The tone of his questions put Claire on guard. Was he still hoping to purchase the property from her?

"Yes, I'm planning to relocate in the winter, Lord willing." She smoothed a strand of hair away from her face. "I've been having repairs done on the house, and will also have the walls painted before I start moving in."

"Wow, I'm sure you're excited. Even though moving can be a chore." His tone was flat, as though he didn't share her enthusiasm. He smiled, but it appeared forced. What was his problem?

Claire fought the idea that he was indeed still interested in purchasing her land. That thought only made her bristle, and she wouldn't be rude to him—especially standing mere feet away from the church building. His next words completely caught her off guard.

"I'm sure you're busy these days, but would you like to have dinner with me sometime before you move? Maybe this Saturday? If you have time." He paused, studying her face, then continued. "We don't know each other well, but since we seem to keep encountering each other, it might be nice to at least be friends." He glanced down at the ground briefly. Where was the confidence he'd exuded in the attorney's office?

Was Dexter asking her on a date? Surely it wasn't so he could discuss her land, was it? If so, she'd set him straight yet again. But…he seemed sincere in wanting to have a casual dinner as a friend. What would be the harm?

Claire moistened her lips and smiled up at him, trying hard to ignore the fact that he was possibly the most handsome man she'd ever seen. "Sure, that sounds nice. Shall I meet you somewhere?" Oops. Maybe she shouldn't have said that, but too late now. After all, women had to be careful—especially if they didn't know their date well.

Dexter was obviously taken aback by her question, but he smiled and shrugged. "If you'd feel more comfortable meeting me at a restaurant, we can do that. But I really don't mind picking you up. It's your decision."

Claire met his gaze. "Okay, why don't you tell me where to meet you, and I'll be there. My apartment is pretty much a jumbled mess right now with my boxes sitting around, so the only person who sees it is Marcy." She didn't miss the amused glint in his eyes as she rambled on. Clearly, she was fumbling in her excuse to meet him rather than have him come for her.

To his credit, he didn't press the issue but grinned. "Okay, that sounds good. How about meeting me at six o'clock on Saturday at the Fernwood Grill—does that sound okay to you?" He'd taken his car keys from his pocket and clasped them in his hand.

"Sure, that sounds good." Her mind raced. Had she done the right thing in accepting his invitation? A sudden thought caused her to blurt out a question. "Do you have my number in case something comes up?" Claire knew she was blushing. Why couldn't she sound more confident?

His eyes widened. "No, I don't, so I'm glad you thought of that. But no worries—nothing will come up on my end. Do you still have my business card with my number? I gave you one the day I…uh, we met at the attorney's office." He took his cell phone out to enter her number.

Claire told him she still had his card, leaving out the detail that she'd looked at it so much it was practically dog-eared. She gave him her number, then they said good-bye and went to their cars. She was relieved he'd parked in a different area because she needed to gather her thoughts. If he'd been walking beside her, he would've been a distraction. A very attractive, interesting distraction. A distraction Claire now had a date with the following Saturday.

~ ~ ~

Well, that wasn't the smoothest experience he'd ever had asking a girl for a date. Dexter practically groaned aloud as he headed to his car after his conversation with Claire. He was thankful his parents had hurried out of church to meet friends for Sunday lunch. What was it about Claire that made him so flustered? At least she'd accepted his invitation for dinner on Saturday, even though he wouldn't be picking her up, but rather meeting her at the restaurant.

Still, it would be a date, and he was eager to spend time with her and learn more about her. She intrigued him, although Dexter wasn't sure exactly why. Maybe the fact that Claire Durham seemed so different from the usual women he'd dated—especially the Fernwood Country Club females.

Heading into his apartment to fix a sandwich, he grinned as he thought about telling Howard. His buddy would be pleased that he'd asked out the lovely landowner. As though picking up his vibes, Howard phoned him seconds later.

"Hey, you want to grab a burger later today and watch the game at my place?" Howard's eager voice came through. The way he sounded caused Dexter to wonder if his friend had some good news of his own.

"Sure, sounds good. I'll grab the burgers on the way and then come to your apartment. Just tell me the time. I'm not sure when the game starts."

After Howard gave him the time, their call ended. Dexter hadn't even given a hint that he had news to share and was still curious if maybe Howard did too. Good grief. His thoughts reminded him of being in middle school again and having a secret crush on the head cheerleader. But you're not in middle school—you're twenty-nine years old. And you need to make a major decision about what to do with your life.

The silent chiding was a startling reminder that he did, in fact, need to make some decisions. Soon. As if on cue, part of the pastor's message from that morning replayed in his mind. *Pray.* The pastor had emphasized how important it was for Christians to pray to make the right decision. Not only in major situations but smaller ones, too. Yet this was a major decision that Dexter needed to make, and he wasn't getting anywhere on his own.

"Okay, Lord. I haven't been in close touch with You these past few years, but I'm trying to do better. I'm not sure what to do, but I need a change in my life. My father has accepted that I no longer want to continue on in his real estate company, and he's good with that. I still enjoy working in real estate, but don't want to follow in his shadow. I want to do something on my own." He spoke the words aloud in a heartfelt prayer, and when he finished, a sense of peace washed over him.

Later, as he and Howard ate and enjoyed the football game on television, Howard shared that he and Liz had officially called it quits, and he was actually relieved. Dexter had to suppress a laugh because it was almost comical listening to his friend—Howard's relief was so obvious.

"So, do you have someone else in mind?" Dexter had

a sneaking suspicion there was more to Howard's story.

"Funny you should ask because I recently reconnected with someone on social media." Howard grinned and waggled his eyebrows. Totally out of character for him, but the gesture was amusing to Dexter.

His friend went on to explain he and an acquaintance from his college chemistry class had been in touch, and she lived in a city about twenty minutes from Fernwood. "I don't want to get my hopes up, but we'll see what happens." Howard took a big bite of his hamburger, as though celebrating his news.

Dexter waited a few minutes before sharing that he'd asked Claire to a dinner date for the upcoming Saturday. Howard's eyes widened and he dropped a French fry. Dexter released a laugh. "Are you that shocked?"

Howard's reply confirmed that he was, indeed, shocked that Dexter had asked Claire on a date. But he also added how happy he was for his friend. "Sounds like both of us might finally be making progress in the dating area. Not that you ever needed to worry." He tossed out the teasing comment as a reminder of their college days when Dexter seldom was without a date.

Wanting to boost his buddy's confidence, Dexter shook his head. "Yeah, but lately I haven't been pushing the females away. Unless you want to count Brittany. Guess she finally got the message that I wasn't interested in a spoiled, immature rich girl." Dexter almost felt a stab of guilt, but he was speaking the truth. He saw no sense in leading on someone who wasn't his type. And Brittany wasn't even close.

Before Dexter left Howard's apartment, his friend poked his arm playfully. "Be sure and let me know how your date goes on Saturday. I'll be eager to hear what happens."

Dexter was glad he hadn't shared that he and Claire were meeting at the restaurant. That detail almost made it seem like less of a date, but at least they'd have time together while they ate. He hoped to learn more about the soft-spoken woman who was planning to move away soon.

At the reminder of Claire's upcoming move, a twinge of regret poked at Dexter. He had a feeling that he may very well end up regretting that he'd not gotten to know her sooner because if they continued dating, the road was long between Fernwood and Peach Grove.

~ ~ ~

Gripping her steering wheel, Claire eased into the parking lot for the Fernwood Grill on Saturday. It didn't matter that she'd reminded herself this was only going to be a casual dinner because her pulse apparently didn't get the message. If only she wasn't so nervous.

Claire and Dexter were supposed to meet at six o'clock, and she'd arrived only a few minutes before the hour. She didn't want to appear overly eager, but didn't want to be late, either. Might as well go inside the restaurant.

She stepped into the building, greeted by a smiling hostess and the tantalizing aroma of steak. Quickly telling the hostess that she was meeting someone, Claire sat on a bench inside the entrance, positioning herself at one end beside a large green plant. Somehow, the plant made her feel less obvious as she waited for Dexter.

Laughter and conversation reached her ears—apparently some of the patrons were having a fun time. Beyond the hostess station were the tables, and most were full. Suddenly Claire's eyes landed on a man leaving one of the tables, and he turned around as though telling the others good-bye. Dexter. Was he here with a group of friends? Had he forgotten his plans with her?

Dexter walked quickly toward the entrance and then spotted Claire, now practically huddled beside the plant. He looked surprised but his face lit up with a welcoming smile. "Claire! I didn't see you come in. I'm so sorry—did you just arrive?"

She slowly stood, clutching her handbag like a security blanket. "Yes, only a few minutes ago."

"Again, I'm so sorry I didn't see you right away. I arrived about ten minutes early and saw a group of friends I went to high school with, so stepped over to say hello. I kept watching the door so I'd see you, but obviously I missed you when you entered." He turned to the hostess, and it was evident he'd spoken with her earlier because she replied that his table had been prepared.

He lightly placed a hand on Claire's back as they

followed the hostess to a small table toward the back of the restaurant. Dexter thanked the woman, then pulled out a chair for Claire before seating himself. Before opening his menu, he apologized yet again for not seeing her when she'd arrived.

"It's fine, really. That's nice you saw some friends from school." She opened her menu, hoping Dexter wouldn't notice her trembling hands. She really needed to calm down so she could enjoy this date. *Date.* Simply thinking the word didn't help calm her, and she almost knocked over her glass of water. Great.

Dexter commented about seeing his friends earlier. "It's funny that many of us went away to college, but returned to the Fernwood area to live and work." He shrugged, then asked if she was from the Fernwood area.

Claire shook her head. "No, but not too far away from here. I grew up in the Roswell area, went to college in Atlanta, but then decided to live and work in Fernwood when my best friend did, too." She laughed lightly. "We went to different colleges, but always kept in touch. I'll miss seeing Marcy often after I move." She must sound pathetic. After all, she wasn't a kid heading out on her own.

"Marcy is the friend who works with you, right?"

Claire smiled. "Yes, she's a great friend."

Their server approached to take their orders. Claire was touched by Dexter's concern that she'd only ordered a bowl of soup, but no way was she admitting she was too nervous to eat much. Now if she could get through this meal without dumping soup in her lap, it'd be successful.

To her relief, their meal went smoothly with conversation flowing easily. Claire learned that Dexter was also an only child and his father was preparing to retire. Surprisingly, Dexter wasn't going to take over his father's business, but another man was purchasing the real estate company. Was it Claire's imagination, or did Dexter seem eager to open up about the family business? That was a silly thought because he still didn't know her well.

As if reading her thoughts, he grinned sheepishly. "You're a good listener, Claire. I didn't mean to bore you with details about my family's future plans."

She shook her head. "You haven't bored me at all. I enjoy hearing about other people's work—it's interesting." She hesitated before continuing. "So…since you don't want to continue in your father's company, what will you do?" She hoped the question didn't sound as though she was prying, yet he'd been the one to share information with her.

He splayed his hands and shrugged. "That's a good question. I'm really not sure. I'd like to continue in real estate, but I—" His sentence was interrupted when the server brought his salad. He looked at Claire, his eyes holding concern. "Are you sure you only wanted soup? We can order a salad for you also, if you'd like. You're hardly eating anything."

She thanked him but assured him she was fine. "I'm

sure the soup will be filling. You go ahead and enjoy your salad." She took another sip of her water, hoping he'd continue with his previous comment.

Before taking a bite of lettuce, he finished his interrupted sentence. "Anyway, I guess I want to do something completely on my own, instead of following in my father's shadow." As soon as he spoke, he quickly put the lettuce in his mouth and chewed, looking a bit uncomfortable.

Claire couldn't help wondering if he'd not meant to make that comment. She felt compelled to put him at ease, so she smiled. "That's admirable. A lot of guys would just go ahead and take over a family business, but if you have the desire to do something completely on your own, that's great."

With obvious relief in his expression, Dexter grinned and thanked her. "I appreciate that because I almost feel guilty at times since I'm not taking over his company. But he's assured me that he wants me to be happy and decide what I really want to do the remainder of my working years." He took another bite.

"Well, there you go, then. It's not as though your father is disappointed or hurt that you're not taking over, so you can pursue something else with a clear conscience." Good grief. When had she become so bold in offering her thoughts so openly? Especially with someone she wasn't close to. *Maybe you'd like to be close to him.* The sudden thought sent a warmth rushing up to her face, and she was relieved their meal had arrived.

The remainder of their time was filled with comments about their food, her job at the logistics company, and llamas. Claire couldn't suppress a giggle when she told Dexter about the neighbor's llamas who grazed in her pasture. "They're adorable, and I'm actually getting attached to them. Of course, I only see them when I visit my house on weekends, but I understand how someone would become very fond of them." She didn't miss the amused gleam in Dexter's eyes.

"Have you ever raised llamas before?" His question sounded sincere, which for some reason gave Claire a warm, fuzzy feeling.

"Never. In fact, I'd only seen pictures of llamas before I saw the ones grazing in my pasture. When the neighbor stopped by to explain the previous landowner had allowed the llamas to graze there, he asked if I minded. Of course, I said, 'no—I think they're cute.'" Yikes. Maybe she was overdoing her exuberance for the creatures.

But Dexter's reaction was reassuring. He seemed to be genuinely interested rather than acting like she was crazy. He even asked more questions about them. But Claire was guarded because she had to make absolutely certain he wasn't still holding out hope she'd sell her land to him. No way was that happening.

"They're really sweet, and are actually domesticated animals. Since llamas came from South America, I was shocked to see a small herd in my pasture in Peach Grove." She laughed, then continued. "I wondered at first if they were alpacas, but those are smaller with short ears. The llamas have a longer face with banana-size ears." *Stop rambling.* Claire grabbed her glass of water and took a sip, hoping Dexter would talk. She'd said more than enough.

He was grinning, but his tone was gentle, not mocking. "Sounds like you've learned a lot about them. I'll admit I've never been around animals much, except for zoo visits as a child and having a dog years ago. I take it that you're fond of animals in general?"

Claire nodded, then proceeded to tell him about her cats, Simon and Isaiah. "Animals are smarter than people might think. It's easy to become attached to them." She clamped her lips together, determined not to babble on about her felines as she'd done with the llamas. Instead, she asked him about his family's holiday plans, hoping to gain more insight into this obviously-wealthy man. She'd even wondered if he and his parents traveled to some exotic location for the holidays.

To Claire's surprise, his response indicated they celebrated the way many families did and hosted relatives for dinner. Could it be her notion of Dexter and his family had been a bit exaggerated? Maybe he wasn't the rich, spoiled son she'd thought he was.

As the couple stood from their chairs a few minutes later, Claire smiled and placed her handbag over her shoulder. "Thank you so much for my delicious meal. I really enjoyed this." She might as well make a polite exit so this wouldn't be awkward.

"At least let me walk you to your car." He placed the money for their meal inside the leather cover holding the check, then added more money which Claire was certain must be a generous tip.

The pair headed outside into the chilly night, and Claire shivered. "It's definitely December." She laughed, then thanked him again for her meal.

They reached her car, and Claire pressed the keypad to unlock her door and quickly climbed inside. When she turned her head to the left, Dexter was leaning slightly down toward her, but not too close. Thankfully he'd not tried to kiss her—this had only been a casual meal together. At least, that's what she'd been telling herself.

Dexter cleared his throat. "I know Christmas is coming and you're busy getting ready to move, but would you like to go out again? If you have time, that is." The parking lot lighting cast shadows on his face, giving him a more ruggedly handsome appearance.

"Sure, that sounds nice." Claire wasn't sure what else to say. She didn't want to sound too eager, but the thought of another date with Dexter made her heart beat faster.

"Okay, I have your number in my phone, so I'll call you soon. Be safe driving to your apartment." He gently closed her car door, then turned to head to his car parked a few spaces away.

Claire headed out of the parking lot to return home,

and had to be careful not to speed. She could hardly wait to scurry inside her apartment and phone Marcy because she was sure her friend was eager to hear the details of Claire's date with Dexter.

Yet, even as she entered her apartment, fed her cats, and prepared to phone Marcy, a question hovered in her mind. Was she being foolish to risk seeing Dexter again, when she was guarding her heart? After all, if he was, in fact, hoping to convince her to sell her land, this might likely break her heart. She couldn't be too careful.

~ ~ ~

As usual, the Fernwood community was lavishly decked out in Christmas finery. Dexter didn't know if it was his imagination or not, but it seemed each year the country club area where his parents lived added more decorations. His mother normally joined in with the other middle-aged ladies helping with the decorating, in addition to the decorations adorning the Jennings' home.

To Dexter's surprise, his mother had casually admitted that this year she wasn't displaying all her customary Christmas décor. She stated this on Sunday afternoon during dinner at the country club. Dexter almost dropped his salad fork when she commented on the fact, and for a few seconds he even wondered if she might be ill.

But she'd laughed at his startled expression, informing him that the fewer decorations she had Geneva to haul up from their basement, the fewer there would be to put away after Christmas. "And since I'm eager for your father and me to begin our travels, putting away ornaments and such will be one less thing to take care of when the holiday season has ended."

Although she made it sound as though she did most of the work, Dexter knew it was Geneva who always handled the majority of it. He merely smiled and nodded, hoping his mother wouldn't go overboard in her travel plans while his father was still regaining his strength.

"Isn't it wonderful that your father's retirement is coinciding with Christmas? The reception Dora is planning for him will have a Christmas theme, she told me. I offered to help her, even though that wouldn't be proper since I'm the guest of honor's wife." She smiled before sipping her tea.

Carl shook his head, playfully frowning at his wife, then shifting his gaze to Dexter. "I've told your mother I don't want a big fuss made. Yes, I've worked hard over the years building my real estate company, but with Neal purchasing the business and taking over, I have a good feeling about the transition."

Dexter remained silent, mixed emotions running through him. His father appeared completely fine with the fact that an acquaintance would purchase and run the real estate company, and Carl never once gave Dexter the impression he was disappointed in his son. So why did Dexter still have that tug of guilt about the matter?

As though reading his thoughts, his mother patted his

hand. "Dexter, dear, have you decided if you're going to remain at the company a while longer? You said you've been undecided what to do, but there's no need to rush into another job if you're not ready. Your father said that Neal made it clear you're welcome to remain there, although your father won't be the owner."

Thankfully, their server arrived with their steak dinners, so Dexter had a couple of minutes to gather his thoughts. He hated admitting to his parents that he was floundering about making a decision. Actually, not even floundering—he had no clue what to do.

As they dug into their steaks, Dexter shrugged. "Not really, mother. I still enjoy real estate, but wonder if I still need a change to do something else."

His father aimed a quizzical frown at him, but his tone was gentle. "There's no need for you to rush, as your mother said. Deciding on a job is a major step, and you want to be happy."

Dexter smiled and thanked his father, then resumed eating. To his relief the remainder of their mealtime talk was about Christmas and his parents' travel plans. But later as he drove to his apartment, Dexter knew he needed to do some serious thinking. And maybe some praying, too. The unexpected thought jolted him. Although he'd been rekindling his relationship with God, Dexter still hadn't been praying as he should. In fact, he'd not even attended church that morning. Was that why he felt a restlessness inside?

He hadn't mentioned his date with Claire to his

parents, but if he continued seeing her, he'd definitely make introductions. Although she wasn't part of their country club, Claire would make a good impression on his mother and father, he was certain.

He entered his apartment—his quiet, lonely apartment. The image of Claire hovered in his thoughts, combined with the recent conversation with his parents about his future employment. How had he reached almost thirty years old and suddenly found himself unsure of his future? The assumption he'd held for years that he'd take over his father's company, get married, and reside in Fernwood—most likely near the country club—now held no appeal. Was he just going through a restless phase, or did he need to do some serious soul-searching?

~ ~ ~

Claire hated that she'd been a bit disappointed not seeing Dexter at church that morning. Her date with him had gone well, and surprisingly she'd ended up enjoying their conversation at the restaurant.

As expected, Marcy had been eager to hear all the details, which Claire shared with her on the phone the previous night. Now as they ate sandwiches at Marcy's apartment after church, her friend seemed intent on continuing the topic.

"So, when do you think you'll hear from him again?" Marcy's eyes twinkled. Her enthusiasm over happenings in Claire's life always amazed Claire. A true friend, and one she'd miss after moving to Peach Grove.

Shrugging, Claire attempted to sound as though it didn't matter. "I'm not sure, but it went well. I feel kind of guilty that I had him pegged as a snobby realtor used to getting what he wants because that's not how I see him at all anymore." She took a bite of her sandwich.

Marcy arched an eyebrow. "Sounds like you've fallen for him after one date."

Claire laughed and shook her head. "No, besides I'm getting ready to move almost two hours away, so this isn't a good time to fall for anyone in Fernwood." Before Marcy could respond, Claire's phone rang.

Her uncle was phoning to give an update on recent repairs at her house. Claire held her breath when Ben told about a few glitches they'd had with some wiring, but then he assured her all was well. How could she ever repay her kind uncle? What a blessing he and her cousin were overseeing the work on her house.

After the call ended, Claire kept the conversation away from Dexter and centered on her house repairs and her decorating ideas. As they chattered about Christmas plans, Claire noticed her friend becoming serious, and she had a sneaking suspicion it had something to do with Tyler.

"Have you heard from Tyler recently?" She asked Marcy gently, hoping he'd not let her down again.

Marcy offered a forced-sounding laugh and shrugged. "Last week he phoned briefly, telling me how busy he was with his job and helping his dad. Sounded like excuses, so I told him I was staying busy these days, too. No dates lined up, which is fine. Claire, I think I've been wasting my time with Tyler. I should've known better than to think he'd changed." She released a long sigh.

Claire reached out and squeezed her arm. "You don't need somebody who's not reliable. You deserve better than that. At least it's Christmas now, and you told me you have special plans with family members over the holidays, so it won't be as though you're sitting home by yourself." She gave her friend a smile, her heart burdened for Marcy.

Marcy brightened and giggled. "Right. And then after the holidays, I'll be busy helping my best friend move to a tiny country town—which I plan on visiting a lot in the future."

Claire laughed, nodding vigorously. "And don't forget one of my spare bedrooms is going to be your special room to stay in when you visit."

That reminder brought a grin to Marcy's face, and she quickly returned to her usual upbeat self. Soon the friends were laughing about funny incidents that had happened at work, and Claire was reminded yet again of what a special friend she had in Marcy.

An hour later, Claire headed to her apartment, thinking of the Christmas cookies she wanted to bake the next week. Up ahead, a sports coupe had pulled out of the Fernwood Country Club development, heading away from her. Dexter. Her pulse raced. Maybe he'd been visiting his parents.

He was alone and likely hadn't seen her. What did it matter? They'd had dinner together the previous evening, but she might never hear from him again. Besides, as she'd told Marcy, she had plenty to do with her upcoming move. Not to mention they were in the Christmas season, and she'd be visiting her relatives in north Georgia before long.

Yet she couldn't deny that a part of her hoped Dexter would phone her. And maybe even ask her for a date—a *real* date this time. Not a casual meeting at a restaurant. After all, he'd mentioned he would call her.

But even if that happened, what if she fell for him? She'd be moving in less than two months. Why had the timing worked out this way?

~ ~ ~

Dexter's phone rang Monday evening, indicating a call from his mother. "Hi, Mom."

"Dear, I've been meaning to remind you that your aunt and uncle will be joining us for Christmas this year, so make sure you'll be in town so you can be with us." She paused, waiting for a response. What she added caused Dexter to inwardly groan.

"I wanted to tell you that if there's anyone special in your life right now, feel free to bring her along to our Christmas dinner. The more the merrier." A forced laugh followed her words.

His mother meant well. She was so eager for him to find someone and settle down. Preferably someone from their Fernwood Country Club or a similar area. Not gonna happen, at least, not in the foreseeable future. He chose his words carefully.

"Thanks, Mom. I'll be joining the family, and look forward to seeing Aunt Sue and Uncle Ed. As for someone special, sorry to disappoint you, but there's no one at the moment. But I appreciate the reminder, and when there is someone special, I'll make sure to let you and Dad know." He chuckled, hoping to keep the conversation light. He didn't want to discuss the lack of romance in his life with his mother, even though he knew she had good intentions.

After the call ended, Dexter found himself thinking about Claire. Again. When they'd had dinner at the Fernwood Grill, Dexter had known for certain that the gentle, soft-spoken lady was genuinely a caring person. Not to mention beautiful. In fact, Claire didn't even realize how beautiful she was. So why was she single? It would have to be by choice because a woman with that many shining qualities wouldn't be unattached due to no interested suitors.

Since Christmas was fast approaching and Claire was planning to move in January, he'd better not waste time if he wanted to get to know her better—even begin a dating relationship with her. But he'd need to be careful because he had a feeling a woman like Claire wouldn't be charmed by a man who seemed overly eager to rush into a relationship. An idea formed, and he hoped it would work out.

The Fernwood Church would hold their annual Christmas Cantata soon. Although he didn't usually attend that event, Dexter decided to invite Claire to join him. Maybe afterward he could take her out to eat. Glancing at the clock, he saw it was already eight-thirty, so he'd just wait and phone her tomorrow.

The next day, he phoned Claire a few minutes before six o'clock. Surely, she'd be home from her job by now. Claire's breathless voice answered, and for a few seconds, Dexter wondered if she'd been running, although she hadn't mentioned being a runner.

"Hi, Claire. Is this a bad time?"

"Hi, Dexter. No, I was feeding my cats and had tuna on my hands, so I hurried to wash them before grabbing the phone." An embarrassed-sounding laugh followed her words.

He chuckled, relieved to know she was in her apartment rather than running beside a busy street. Getting right to the point, he mentioned the choir's performance and asked if she'd like to attend with him.

"Oh...yes, that sounds nice. To be honest, it had slipped my mind that the church choir was doing that. But I love Christmas—and Christmas music—so I'd enjoy that." At least she sounded sincere.

He was prepared for her to say she'd meet him at the church, but he jumped in to say he'd be happy to pick her up, suggesting a time. Practically holding his breath, Dexter was relieved when she replied that would be fine, then gave him her apartment address.

After a few minutes of conversation about Christmas approaching, the call ended. Dexter couldn't deny the warm glow growing inside. He was being ridiculous. This would be a simple date. At least he'd be attending a church event, so maybe this was a good step toward restoring his relationship with God. A guilty jab reminded him he'd need to keep his mind focused on the music's message during the cantata. But with a beautiful woman by his side, that might be a challenge.

~ ~ ~

Wednesday morning at work, Claire grinned and shook her head as Marcy squealed in delight. Her best friend was even more excited about her upcoming date than she was. "I don't know if I should call it a date because what it amounts to is Dexter giving me a ride to church. Although he did mention that if I liked, we'd eat afterwards."

"Girl! That is totally a date. With that incredibly handsome man." Marcy looked about to swoon as she took her canned cola from the drink machine. Just then a few other employees stepped into the breakroom, so the women didn't continue discussing Claire's date.

Claire knew she mustn't allow herself to get sidetracked with thoughts of Dexter. After all, it was almost Christmas and she had an upcoming move to plan for. Yet, she couldn't stop her mind from drifting to the good-looking realtor, and more than once she had to delete incorrect data entries she'd made and enter them again.

That evening while Claire packed another box for her move, her uncle phoned. "Claire-Bear, just letting you know that Jeff and I will be heading to your Peach Grove house this Saturday, and I didn't want you to be startled if you're there and hear us pull in." He chuckled heartily, then added details of a few things they hoped to accomplish while there.

"Thank you, Uncle Ben. I hope you and Jeff aren't going to too much trouble—it's a long drive from Ellijay to Peach Grove."

He assured her they were happy to help, and eager for her to be able to move in. Then Aunt Molly wanted to chat for a few minutes, so they discussed Christmas plans.

When Claire clicked off her phone, a ripple of excitement ran through her. Being with her relatives for Christmas, then moving into her house later in the winter were major events for her—happy events.

But underneath her excitement, apprehension loomed. The doubts tried to resurface again. What if she didn't like living in the small, rural community? What would she do for work? She couldn't live off her savings forever. And her biggest fear of all seemed to taunt her. What if she was lonely? At least she didn't struggle with the fear as she had in previous years, after the stalking incidents. She shuddered and pushed the awful memories from her mind.

As if on cue, a soft meow sounded, and she glanced down to see Simon gazing up at her. She scooped up the striped feline, cuddling him in her arms. "I know, fella. As long as I have you and Isaiah, I won't be lonely. And the llamas." She giggled at the thought of the cute critters who grazed in her pasture. Claire hoped her neighbor would continue bringing the llamas to graze because she always enjoyed seeing them. Their cute faces and banana-shaped ears always made her smile.

The next morning at work, Claire and Marcy stood in the breakroom, admiring the treats on the long table. "This is my favorite time of year in this office." Marcy giggled as she glanced hungrily at the plates of decorated Christmas cookies, small bowls of candy, and a platter with cupcakes.

Claire nodded, picking up a sugar cookie topped with green icing and sprinkles. "Oh, I wanted to let you know I'm heading to Peach Grove this Saturday, if you want to join me." She took a bite of the cookie, savoring the gooey icing on her tongue.

Marcy sighed and shook her head. "I wish I could. My brother and his wife want me to join them for an early supper at their house, but I have a sneaking suspicion it's a sympathy meal." She reached for a gingerbread cookie.

"A sympathy meal? Did someone pass away?"

Marcy's chuckle relieved Claire's concern. "No, I just mean that they feel sorry for me since my relationship with Tyler didn't work out. The creep." She shook her head. "Anyway, I'm now the pitiful spinster in my family."

"Hey, you're not a pitiful spinster. Besides, if you're one, that makes me one, too. Nope. We are not pitiful spinsters. Period." Claire grinned, grabbed another cookie, and headed for the door. "I'd better get back to work. When I leave this job, I want to make sure I'm all caught up."

Her mind wasn't on the data she needed to enter for her job. Instead, she replayed Marcy's comments about being a spinster. Claire couldn't help wondering if she and her friend were destined to remain single forever. An image of Dexter popped into her head, and before she realized it, her mind whirled with thoughts of what it would be like to continue dating him, and maybe even have a future with him.

Whoa! Where were these thoughts coming from? She'd only had one dinner with him, and this Sunday they'd attend the Christmas cantata together. Two "dates" shouldn't invite thoughts of a future with the handsome man. She grabbed the Christmas cookie and took another bite. Maybe having some sugar would jolt sense into her. No way would she be caught up in daydreams of the man who'd wanted to purchase her land. After all, there was still much she didn't know about him.

Yet deep inside, she yearned to continue seeing him, and if that led to a lasting relationship, then so be it. A male voice sounded from her office doorway, and Claire's head jerked.

Her boss clutched a folder of papers, his eyes twinkling. "I hope I didn't startle you, Claire, but with that smile on your face, it appears you're having a wonderful day."

A dreaded blush heated her face, and she wiped cookie crumbs off her mouth. "It's such a festive time of year—I guess everyone is smiling." *Oh boy, could I possibly say anything cheesier?* Better keep her mouth closed unless he asked her a direct question.

"I was just bringing this folder to you. It's the papers on the Morton project, and you'd graciously offered to look over these figures and enter them. Please make any needed corrections. No rush, but if you could have this completed by the first of the new year it would be great."

"Yes, sir. Not a problem." She smiled sweetly, hoping he'd leave before she blurted out another silly comment. Thankfully, he did.

Claire resumed her typing, but made a mental note to keep thoughts of Dexter Jennings at bay while she was working. Or at the very least, be ready with a sensible response if caught off guard again.

~ ~ ~

Business matters pertaining to his father's impending

retirement filled the following week. Dora was going full speed ahead with plans for the lavish retirement reception and several times consulted Dexter for his advice about Carl's favorite foods. The Jennings' housekeeper had also offered her help and planned on preparing some of the food. The reception would be held the following Sunday afternoon, which was only a few days before Christmas.

Everyone around Dexter appeared to be in a festive mood, and he was getting caught up in the holiday spirit, too. Yet, he couldn't help thinking his spirit would feel even lighter if he and Claire actually had a real relationship, rather than a few casual dates before she moved. Dexter had phoned her a couple of times but had gotten her voice mail. Why hadn't he left a message for her? After all, their time together at the Christmas Cantata had been relaxed and enjoyable, with no awkward moments. Yes, he should've left a message on her voice mail.

Well, he had more than enough to keep him busy at the moment. Dexter and his father met with Neal at the country club on Thursday, and Neal again reminded Dexter he could stay on at the real estate company as long as he'd like. In fact, the new owner of the real estate company even told Dexter that it would be helpful if he planned to remain there at least a few months.

After their meeting, Carl commented to Dexter on their drive home. "Neal is hoping you'll stay on a while, son. He's mentioned a few projects that he'll need your help with, and I could tell he's sincere."

When Dexter returned to his apartment a while later, he mulled over what Neal had said. At least that would provide income while Dexter decided what he wanted to do, and he'd be helping Neal at the same time. The man had been a good friend to his father, so it would be the right thing to do. Maybe his future didn't look as bleak as he'd thought.

On that note, he decided to try again to phone Claire. To his relief, she answered this time. "Hey, Claire. Are you still at work?" Christmas music played in the background. Was her office was having a party?

She laughed. "No, I'm in my apartment baking Christmas cookies, and I'm playing some holiday music. It's just something I do each year." Her soft voice sounded light and cheery, making Dexter smile.

"Sounds like a nice tradition. I just didn't want to catch you at work, but thought I'd call before you head out of town for Christmas. You have a lot to do with your move and all, but I'd like to see you if you have time. Maybe the week after Christmas? I could even help you pack, if you need me to." Hopefully he didn't sound desperate, but he really wanted to see her again.

Her tone registered surprise, and she giggled. "That's very kind, but you don't need to help me pack. I do appreciate the offer, though."

"Okay, well…would you have time to go out to dinner one evening the week after Christmas?" If she turned him down, he'd have to assume she wasn't interested. That thought sent a punch to his gut.

"That sounds nice. Oops, my oven timer just buzzed, so I'd better grab the cookies before they burn."

"Sure, I'll let you go. Have a great Christmas, Claire, and I'll call soon."

She wished him a merry Christmas, and the call ended.

Disappointment coursed through Dexter. At least she sounded agreeable to having dinner with him again, so he could look forward to another date with her. He'd just hoped their conversation would last longer.

Snap out of it, Jennings. You have presents to buy. In addition to purchasing Christmas gifts for his parents, he needed to buy a retirement gift for his father. Yeah, he didn't have time to mope because life was moving fast these days, and besides—it was the Christmas season. And maybe next Christmas would be different. After all, a guy could dream.

~ ~ ~

Claire thoroughly enjoyed being with her relatives during Christmas and was humbled at the gifts they'd bestowed on her. They'd truly gone overboard this year, and Claire was certain it was due to her move. No longer would she occupy a tiny, one-bedroom apartment, but an entire house.

Her aunt and uncle even gave presents for her cats, including catnip toys and food. Claire loved every minute of being with them, which made it harder to return to Fernwood. Yet Uncle Ben reminded her that they would see her again when he and Jeff came to check on repairs in her house.

Before Claire left their home the day after Christmas, Aunt Molly pulled her aside and gazed directly into her eyes. "Sweetie, we're thrilled about your plans to move, and know you're going to make that house into a beautiful home. But are you sure you'll be okay? Living in a different community all alone? We don't want you to be fearful—ever." Molly clasped Claire's hands.

Claire knew why her aunt was expressing concern, even without stating the obvious. After being stalked by a man while she was in college, Claire had lived always looking over her shoulder for the next year. But it turned out that the man who stalked her had mistaken her for another woman. Then, a month after that ordeal ended, he took his own life. Sad, but Claire's relatives were relieved that she no longer had to contend with the possibility that he might return and stalk her again.

To add to her stress, Claire had lost her mother the year before the stalking, so she dealt with grief in addition to fear. After counseling sessions, finishing her college degree, and then moving to Fernwood, Claire had been doing well. Now she could read the genuine concern in Molly's eyes.

"You're so sweet to fret about me, Aunt Molly, but I promise you I'm fine. Really." She paused, giving her aunt a smile that she hoped would let her know she *was* fine.

Molly nodded, then leaned in closer. "What about the guy you dated a while back? He hasn't caused problems, has he?" A protective tone underscored her words.

"No, thankfully. Kyle was not right for me, so I ended our relationship after only a few months. He phoned me a couple of times after we stopped dating, but then he got the message. No worries—I promise I'm okay now." Claire gave her aunt a wide smile, thankful that she had someone so caring in her life.

Apparently convinced, Molly released Claire's hands but leaned over for a hug. "Just remember your uncle, cousin, and I are always here for you, Claire-Bear."

Claire fought the lump that was forming in her throat. If she became emotional, it might worry her aunt again, so she needed to keep things light. "I appreciate you all so much and can't wait until I'm living in my house and can invite you for a visit."

About fifteen minutes later, Claire was on the road, headed back to Fernwood. She hadn't mentioned Dexter to her aunt, but if she continued dating him, she definitely would. A grin formed at the thought of the contrast between Dexter and her cousin, Jeff. An image of Dexter in an expensive men's suit formed in her thoughts, while an image of Jeff consisted of her cousin in jeans and a flannel shirt. Dexter was city; Jeff was country. Yet, she thought they'd likely hit it off, should they ever meet.

Marcy phoned minutes after Claire stepped into her apartment, eager to hear about her Christmas at Molly's and Ben's and assuring her the cats had been fine the few days Claire was away. "I could tell they missed you, but they know their Aunt Marcy." She and Claire both laughed.

"If you're not busy, you could come over this afternoon while I'm packing another box. I'm almost finished and now have a lovely wall of packed boxes in my living room. At least the furniture can't be packed up, so we won't have to sit on the floor."

"Okay, I'll grab some sandwiches at the Fernwood Deli and be there in a bit. I'm just thankful we have a few days off before we have to return to work."

An hour later, the women enjoyed sandwiches at Claire's kitchen table and each shared about their Christmas with relatives. When Claire's phone rang, it sent a tingle running through her, as she couldn't help wondering if it might be Dexter.

Sure enough, his voice came through, and her face turned crimson as Marcy observed her with a wide grin and mischievous eyes. When he asked her for a dinner date that Friday, she accepted but politely let him know Marcy was visiting at the moment. "She brought supper and is helping me pack." To her relief, he said he hadn't realized she had company, and he'd pick her up on Friday.

"Was that who I think it was?" Marcy leaned across the table, eyes about to burst.

"Yes, and he's taking me to dinner on Friday."

"Girlfriend, you don't sound too happy about it. We *are* talking about the same gorgeous guy, right?" Marcy was eyeing Claire as though she'd lost her mind.

"Yes, Dexter Jennings. But I don't want to do the wrong thing. Why is the timing working out like this? I'm preparing to move out of town, and now suddenly I have a handsome man here in Fernwood asking me for dates." Claire shook her head.

Marcy appeared to ponder this for a moment then stunned Claire with her soft response. "I'll tell you what my mom always tells me. Pray about it. Maybe this is how the timing is supposed to work out. She always reminds me that God's timing is best, even if we don't realize it at the time." Marcy stopped speaking and grabbed her cola, taking a long sip.

Her best friend's words sunk in, and she was right. At this moment, the Lord was using Marcy to remind Claire of a very important truth. A niggle of guilt ran through her that she wasn't trusting—or praying—nearly enough. Because in her heart, she knew that God's timing was perfect, and He would guide her.

~ ~ ~

Dexter couldn't believe all the changes happening in his life. He supposed this new year was going to be vastly different from his past years since reaching adulthood. His father had officially retired, and the reception had gone well, followed by Christmas three days later. Dexter's only regret was he'd thought about Claire most of the time, wondering what it would be like having her at his side for special events. *Or just any old day.*

His date with Claire the week after Christmas went well, and in between bites of steak she'd excitedly updated him on plans for her Peach Grove house. Yet she also wanted to hear about his holidays and plans for his career.

"If you don't have plans for New Year's Eve, we could grab a bite and join the festivities on the Fernwood town square." He grinned, not missing the look of surprise she gave him.

"Are you serious?" She'd asked. Her tone was sincere, not sarcastic.

He nodded, deciding from her reaction she had likely never participated in the event. "Yeah, unless you'd rather not. It's mainly for the younger crowd—you know, those under forty." He laughed, then explained there would be live music, small tents set up selling appetizers and drinks, and at midnight everyone would cheer when the new year began.

"I've only attended once, but it was kind of fun. We don't have to do that—it's just a suggestion." He smiled, not wanting to blow his chances at another date with her. How could he have become so captivated by this woman he'd not known long at all? But he couldn't deny it, and now that she'd be moving soon, he wanted to see her as often as possible.

After considering his offer for a few seconds, Claire brightened. "Sure, that sounds fun. And since I'm moving out of Fernwood, I may as well celebrate in style." She giggled, and he found himself mesmerized by her mannerisms. But when a shadow flitted across her features, he worried.

"What's wrong? Did you change your mind? That's okay if you did—we can do something else."

She shook her head and smiled. "No, your suggestion sounds fun, really it does. I was thinking about my friend Marcy." Claire blew out a sigh, and if Dexter wasn't mistaken, even appeared embarrassed. "I'd told her since this was my last New Year's Eve in Fernwood, that maybe we'd celebrate together. She recently stopped dating a guy she'd been seeing a while, so I've been concerned about her."

Without giving the matter any thought, Dexter blurted out, "Well, my buddy, Howard, also stopped dating someone recently, so maybe your friend and Howard could join us." Did he just say that? Dexter normally didn't play matchmaker for others. But Howard was available, since nothing had developed with his college friend.

"Hmm, that might be an idea. Do you mind telling me a little bit about Howard? So I can tell Marcy."

After they'd both shared a little about their friends, they agreed that Marcy and Howard didn't seem to have much in common, but this gathering was only for one night. "Sometimes opposites attract. At least that's what

I've always heard." Dexter grinned.

Two nights later, Claire and Marcy met up with Dexter and Howard in front of the Fernwood Bistro. They'd agreed that keeping things casual would be the least awkward for their friends. There was a festive atmosphere as music played and people milled around, chatting and laughing.

To Dexter's great relief, Howard and Marcy actually hit it off, although the first few minutes had been a little formal. After that, the party atmosphere of celebrating a brand-new year seemed to lighten up everyone, and the four adults nabbed a small table away from the band so they could actually hear each other speaking.

But the majority of Dexter's attention was focused on the beautiful woman at his side. He watched her listen attentively to Howard telling about his job, and Dexter was again struck with the realization of how much he yearned for a relationship with her. The only problem was the fact she'd be moving in less than a month.

Later that night, the crowd counted down as the last ten seconds of the year gave way to a brand-new year. Dexter couldn't hold back, and he gently turned Claire toward him and gazed into her blue eyes. Eyes that reminded him of the ocean when he'd visited Key West five months earlier. Just as the fireworks began at the stroke of midnight, Dexter placed a sweet kiss on her lips. She didn't pull away, nor did the kiss last long.

But Dexter knew in that moment that he didn't want to stop seeing Claire Durham, no matter how far away she moved. Was it possible for him to find a job in a tiny, rural community that was named for Georgia's favorite fruit?

~ ~ ~

"How could my life go from one extreme to the other?" Claire asked the question aloud in mid-January while taping up the last box ready to be moved to her new house. But her felines offered no answer, and both continued their snoozing on the sofa.

Only a few months earlier, her life had been slower paced, and she'd prayed for the Lord to show her what to do. She'd been content living in Fernwood, working at the logistics company. Yet a restlessness stirred within her, as though she needed to do more. Well, her life was changing in a major way, and she was both thankful and terrified at the same time.

The phone rang at that moment, halting her musings. "Hey, Marcy. Thanks again for helping with my party at the office today. I didn't expect that, and y'all went overboard." Claire fought the emotion rising inside, determined not to cry as she'd done that day when her co-workers surprised her. Even her boss had given a kind speech, complimenting Claire and saying she'd be missed.

Marcy was also feeling emotional at the realization that Claire's moving day was soon. Very soon. Her friend sniffled, then a forced laugh sounded.

"Hey, you deserved that party." Another sniffle sounded, then in true Marcy fashion, she giggled. "I just wanted to make sure you took home enough food from the party. I don't want my best friend going hungry."

"Are you kidding? You packed up so much cake for me, not to mention the other goodies, I won't have to visit the Fernwood stores again." Yet, even as she spoke the words in an attempt to keep the conversation light, she knew it was true. She'd be moving from an upscale Atlanta suburb to a tiny farming community, where she hardly knew anyone, except for Boyd Felton and his sweet wife. Claire had been delighted to meet Maybelle Felton when the couple stopped by her house the previous Saturday to welcome her.

"What can I do to help you? Howard's picking me up Saturday and we'll head to your house to help you move in. But before then if there's something I can do, please call me."

Claire grinned at Marcy referring to Howard. What a blessing that those two had hit it off only two weeks ago at the New Year's Eve celebration on the Fernwood square. Claire had also been thrilled when Dexter surprised her with a sweet kiss at midnight, and she'd realized her feelings for him were more than just a physical attraction.

"I'll call if there's something I need help with, Marcy. But you'd better remember that I'm still going to need our phone visits after I move, so save some time for me when you're busy dating Howard." Claire knew her comment would bring a delighted squeal from Marcy, and it did.

"Girl, I still can't believe I'm dating Dexter's best friend. What are the odds I'd fall for a serious, nerd-type guy?" She cackled, then assured Claire she'd be fine.

"Speaking of Dexter, he's at my door. I invited him to help me eat some of the food from my party at work." A tingle rushed through Claire as she headed toward her front door, after she said good-bye to Marcy.

Dexter greeted her with a wide smile, then noticed the phone in her hand. "Did I interrupt a call?"

"No, it was Marcy checking on me, and we were about to end the call. Come on in and help yourself to this spread." She laughed and gestured to the food on her kitchen counter.

"Wow. Your office went all out. But you deserved it, and they'll miss you." He hesitated, then his voice lowered. "I'll miss you too, Claire, but I'm determined to see you as often as I can. If that's okay with you." His eyebrows rose, as though wanting to make sure she felt the same.

"Sure. I just wish it weren't such a long drive between Fernwood and Peach Grove." She still blushed at times when he looked at her. When he nodded but didn't smile, Claire knew she must keep things light. "Here, let's eat." She grinned and slid a plate of gourmet party sandwiches toward him.

Although she cared deeply for Dexter, she had to keep things in perspective. They would be living two hours apart, so she couldn't be pining after him. She must focus on her moving details and arrangements, not dwell on how much she cared for a good-looking man in Fernwood. After all, she was moving on Saturday and couldn't allow herself to be emotionally drained for her moving day. She needed every bit of strength she could muster.

~ ~ ~

Chapter 10

Moving day had come and gone, leaving Claire exhausted and filled with a whirl of emotions. She couldn't believe she and her cats had moved from the small apartment to a large, two-story house. When she awakened on Sunday morning, Claire wondered if she was dreaming. No, the smell of recently painted walls reminded her that she had, in fact, moved into the house she'd inherited in Peach Grove.

She looked out one of her upstairs windows toward the empty pasture but smiled knowing the llamas would be in the pasture later on. A soft meow from her doorway caused Claire to turn away from the window. Both her cats were getting used to their new home, exploring and sniffing out various rooms. This house must seem like a mansion to her felines, but in time they'd be content there—not to mention having plenty of windows to view the birds outside.

"Okay, let's head downstairs to the kitchen for some tuna. Our first breakfast in our new home calls for a special treat." She grinned as both cats accompanied her down the stairs to the large kitchen, where she enjoyed coffee and doughnuts while her felines ate tuna.

Dexter had told her he'd phone every day to check on her, and he planned to visit the next weekend, along with Marcy and Howard. They'd all insisted they return and help her settle in.

Claire now had no doubts at all that she'd done the right thing in making this move and again thought of her favorite Bible verse in the book of Proverbs. Yes, the Lord had certainly shown her the right paths to take. Even her worries about employment possibilities were working out, as Maybelle Felton had told her their community church needed a secretary to fill in while the regular one was on maternity leave. The pay wouldn't be much, but it would help.

Surprisingly, her week flew by with unpacking, learning her way around the rural area, and enjoying visits from the pastor, his wife, and a few other Peach Grove residents, all welcoming her to the area and offering help should she need it. She felt blessed and looked forward to Saturday, when Dexter, Marcy, and Howard would visit.

Her guests arrived a little after eleven o'clock on Saturday, each of them greeting her with a warm hug. Even shy Howard bestowed a quick, awkward hug, telling her he was impressed with how nice her house already looked.

With chatter, laughter, and endless cups of coffee, the friends worked on hanging pictures, unpacking books and figurines, and then enjoyed pizza that Dexter and Howard picked up from the small Peach Grove pizzeria. Contentment whispered through Claire now that she was finally here.

About five o'clock, Howard and Marcy headed back to Fernwood in Howard's car, but Dexter insisted he'd stay until that night, then head back around ten o'clock. The winter sky was darkening, and the late January air held a chill, but inside Claire's house, the soft glow of lamps and scented candles offered a cozy warmth.

Dexter told Claire even though it was a Saturday, he needed to return a work-related call to Neal, the new owner of his father's real estate company who was allowing him to continue working there. He stepped into the living room as Claire busied herself in the kitchen.

A few minutes later, she couldn't help overhearing a portion of his conversation, and what she heard caused her pulse to quicken. Dexter's voice, in a serious tone drifted to her ears.

"Yeah, I think maybe she'll still sell. It's taking time, but I'm not giving up. We've been working on this for too long to stop pursuing it. This is some prime acreage we're looking at."

The blood drained out of her face, and she hurried to a kitchen chair and sat, pretending to be busy folding a small towel. Her hands shook. Surely, she was mistaken. Surely Dexter wasn't still trying to convince her to sell her land. Yet everything he'd said seemed to indicate he was indeed—he referred to her land. But why? It made no sense. He'd even helped her move and get settled, so why would he do this if he hoped to buy the property?

The talking had stopped, and approaching footsteps let her know he was heading into the kitchen. "Claire? Where are you?"

"I-In the kitchen." She spoke numbly, refolding the kitchen towel yet again.

"Hey, sorry about that work call, but in real estate, business never stops." He gave a slight chuckle, then eyed her closely. "Are you okay? You look pale. Do you feel all right?"

She shook her head and stood. "No, I...I think the pizza didn't agree with me, so I need to take some medicine and rest. You can head back to Fernwood because if this is contagious, you don't need to catch it." Claire didn't miss his worried frown as he gazed at her with his dark eyes. Those eyes that had seemed so attractive: now held deceit. How dumb did he think she was?

"If it's the pizza, I don't think you'd be contagious. But if you're not feeling well, I'll leave so you can rest. Are you sure you'll be okay? If you need me to stay, I will. I'd do anything for you, Claire." He'd reached out and lightly touched her shoulder.

She wrapped her arms around her stomach and shook her head. "You don't need to stay. I'll be okay. Thanks for the pizza and your help." She couldn't even bring herself to look him in the eye again.

Dexter slowly put on his jacket, still eyeing her

warily. Then he held up his cell phone. "Please phone if you need me. I can turn around and head back here."

She nodded, then gave him a weak wave as he stepped onto her front porch, his shoulders uncharacteristically slumped. It was clear he'd not been convinced she was feeling sick.

But Claire didn't care. How could she have been so foolish? She'd thought Dexter Jennings was different, that he really cared about her. That she misjudged him and he wasn't the wealthy real estate agent accustomed to getting his own way. But apparently, she was correct in her original assumption. He used her, still hoping to convince her to sell her property so he could build who knows what on her land.

The tears flowed and her shoulders shook. Claire should've known the wonderful weeks she had recently enjoyed would abruptly end. It didn't matter that she'd moved past her fears from being stalked. Just when she thought there was a decent man she could trust, she was deceived. Finally giving in to exhaustion, Claire slept through the night, awaking the next morning with puffy eyes and feeling emotionally drained. What was happening to her?

~ ~ ~

Slowly pushing from her bed, Claire gave herself a mental pep talk. She must not wallow in her current mood but needed to move on with her life. The Lord had given her a new start in a new place, and it was up to her to make the best of it. She fed her cats, drank coffee, and read her morning devotional. Originally, she'd thought about attending the community church, but with her puffy eyes it might be best to attend next week.

At least the sun was shining on this late January morning, so Claire dressed warmly, grabbed her camera, and headed out to the pasture to visit the llamas. Maybe she could capture a few photos of her new four-legged friends.

As though recognizing her, a few of the llamas trotted toward the fence, and for a minute Claire wondered if they were sending her a message. Maybe they sensed she was upset, and they were offering comfort. *Okay, maybe I'm really losing it.* But as she reached out to pet one of the llamas, Claire was struck with how much she was drawn to these creatures. Was it possible for a person to love llamas?

She opened her camera, adjusted the lens, and began snapping photos. The morning sunlight made it a bit tricky, but she was certain at least a few of the photos would turn out.

Replacing the lens cover, Claire continued petting and talking to the llamas. Then her hand froze at the sound of a car in her driveway. A familiar-sounding car. *No. Go away.* She knew before turning around it was Dexter, and she was right.

He walked toward her, grinning, and looking way too handsome. But she told herself he deceived her, and there was no way she should trust him.

"Good morning. I see you're having a church service with the llamas." His attempt at a lighthearted comment almost brought a smile to her lips, but Claire fought it.

"They're sweet animals and are always glad to see me. I snapped some photos of them." She clamped her mouth closed. She didn't need to offer him an explanation.

"Are you feeling better? I've been so worried about you, so instead of phoning I decided to drive back down here." He reached out and smoothed a strand of hair from her face.

She flinched, noticing his look of surprise. If he was going to sweet-talk her and think she'd eventually sell her land, he was mistaken. He may as well go ahead and leave.

Silence hung in the air, and finally Dexter asked if she was ready to head inside. She wouldn't be rude and tell him he wasn't welcome, so Claire simply nodded. She waved to the llamas, then headed to her door, Dexter following at her heels. How long was he planning to stay? She didn't have anything to say to him.

Taking off his jacket inside the house, Dexter smiled hesitantly at her. "I'm glad to see you're feeling better because I was worried about you. Can I get anything for you while I'm here? I could pick up lunch from Retha's Diner and we could eat here."

Normally, that would've pleased her. But not now. Now that Claire realized what Dexter was doing, there was no way she wanted to share a meal with him. Sure, she'd have to eat, but she would fix something for herself. To eat alone. Claire shook her head but didn't speak.

As he continued staring at her, Claire fought the tears again threatening in her eyes. How could she have any tears left in her? She didn't miss the tender gaze he was giving her, weakening her defenses.

Reaching a hand out, Dexter gently touched her cheek. "Claire, I really have been worried about you. We've only been dating a short time, but in that time, I've developed strong feelings for you. You're so different from any of the women I've dated in the past, and that's a compliment. You're special. So kind and compassionate, caring about everyone. Even animals. You've even gotten me thinking those llamas are cute." He released a chuckle, but Claire remained silent, eyes lowered.

"Driving home last night, I realized something that startled me. I love you, Claire. That's why I had to see you for myself and make sure you're okay."

She looked up at him, her heart pounding and eyes brimming with unshed tears. "You *love* me? How dare you! You don't love me, Dexter Jennings. You love my land, and you're determined to buy it. And I was foolish enough to think I'd misjudged you—that you're not a spoiled, wealthy realtor, accustomed to getting whatever he wants. No, I was right, after all. And you're still determined to seize my land." She clamped her mouth closed, tears streaming down her cheeks.

Dexter stood, mouth ajar, staring at her. It was obvious he was stunned by her words, and he shook his head. "Whatever are you talking about? Determined to get your land?" He shook his head again, clearly confused.

She blinked back the flow of tears so she could speak, although at the moment she only wanted him to be gone. "Yes, I heard you on your phone call last night when I was in the kitchen. I wasn't trying to listen but couldn't help hearing your words. You're not giving up because this is prime acreage." She practically spat the words at him.

Realization suddenly dawned in his eyes, and a smile stretched across his mouth. "My phone call with my new boss? That's what you're referring to? It wasn't about your land, Claire. It's some property Neal found a while back and suggested I look into it. It's not even in Peach Grove, it's near Milledgeville. Neal was afraid if we didn't follow up, another company would buy it." He shook his head again.

Was he telling the truth? Claire wanted to believe him, but wasn't sure what to believe anymore. She allowed him to embrace her but kept her arms by her side.

"Sweetheart, I'd never deceive you. Yes, I'm a real estate professional and used to making deals, but I am honest. My father instilled integrity in me, as all real estate professionals should have." He paused and drew back, studying her eyes. "I'm so very, very sorry that you thought I was on the phone about your property. No, this is your land, and your house, and I couldn't be happier for you. Well, except that you're too far from Fernwood." He wiped away her tears with his thumb, then planted a kiss on her lips.

She didn't resist. In fact, it was a wonder she was still standing. As though sensing her tiredness, Dexter gently led her to the table, then poured a cup of coffee from her coffeepot and set it in front of her.

"I want you to sit here and drink some coffee, and I'm going to pick up food at Retha's Diner. I shouldn't be gone long, and then we'll eat. Do you want fried chicken, meat loaf, or all vegetables?" He grinned at her, again smoothing hair off her face.

She looked up at him with relieved eyes. "Surprise me." Then she took a sip of coffee, letting the warmth soothe her parched throat and offer comfort to her soul.

Less than thirty minutes later, the couple sat at Claire's table, sunshine streaming in as they ate their fried chicken dinners. Dexter had even brought extra pieces of chicken for Simon and Isaiah, and the felines gazed adoringly up at him. He continued watching her closely, as though wanting to make sure she was okay.

Claire prayed while Dexter was gone to the diner. She'd jumped to conclusions, and she needed to apologize, but also it was time for her to open up to him about her past fears due to the stalking. Not to gain sympathy from him, but so he'd understand what she lived with in her past.

When their meal was finished, Claire went ahead and told Dexter a brief version of what she'd endured her last year of college. "It was a long time before I could trust any man again." She reached up and twirled a strand of her hair.

Dexter's eyes held such compassion that Claire wondered if he was going to cry. Thankfully, he didn't. But his eyes flashed, and he told her it was a good thing the stalker was no longer alive. A protective tone was evident in his words and his mannerisms. He reached over and clasped her hand in his, then placed his other hand on top.

"I didn't share that for sympathy, only so you'd know my background."

He leaned closer to her, shaking his head. "I know you're not trying to garner sympathy, but no woman should ever go through something so horrific. I'm sorry, Claire, so very sorry you endured that." He drew in a deep breath, and his next words sent tingles to the tips of her toes. "As long as I'm living, no man will ever threaten you again, in any way." The determined gaze of his coal-dark eyes let Claire know he was sincere.

~ ~ ~

Chapter 11

Valentine's Day arrived, a crisp, sunny day that sent a spark of energy through Claire. She was settling nicely into her home, pleased with the decorative touches she was gradually adding. She'd even ordered some new furniture that would be delivered soon, and Claire couldn't wait to fix up her extra bedrooms—especially the one she'd designated as Marcy's room.

Claire's part-time job as church secretary was going well, providing her with income while enabling her to meet members of the congregation. She knew she would be happy attending the Peach Grove Christian Church and looked forward to helping in many church activities.

Even her photography was going well, as word spread that she enjoyed taking photos of animals and nature, and one couple had even contacted her about taking photos at a birthday party. She was hesitant at first, but after accepting their offer for the child's sixth birthday party, she realized how much she enjoyed interacting with the children. The happy parents said they'd recommend her to their friends with young children.

Since it was Valentine's Day, Claire had placed a bright red bow on a fence pos, and snapped a few llama photos. She couldn't resist, and even the llamas appeared to enjoy the attention. Afterwards, she hurried into her house to freshen up before Dexter arrived for a Valentine's Day lunch.

She'd offered to cook a meal for him, but he'd insisted he would pick up food from Retha's Diner and bring it to her house. Then they could spend the afternoon together. Claire put on her favorite pink sweater and lit some scented candles. She was so thankful their relationship had continued, especially after the horrible misunderstanding in January.

A few minutes after noon, Claire rushed to her front door as soon as the bell rang. Dexter stood on her porch, grinning and holding the boxed meals from the diner. How could the man look more handsome each time she saw him? And smell better. His musky cologne drifted to Claire's nose as she invited him into the house.

But after setting the meals on her kitchen table, Dexter's brow furrowed, and he gestured toward the back door. "Before we eat, let's go out to the llamas because I noticed something when I pulled in your driveway." His tone was serious, causing Claire's pulse to quicken.

"Is something wrong? I was just out with them earlier, snapping photos. They all appeared just fine." She hurried out her back door with Dexter, hoping one of the beloved critters wasn't injured.

Dexter grasped her hand, causing further concern in Claire. Was he trying to prepare her, in case something was seriously wrong? He knew how much she cared about the llamas.

Claire gazed at the pasture, silently counting the llamas. They were all there and appeared to be just fine. What had Dexter noticed that caused concern?

Before she could question him, Dexter pointed toward a fencepost. "See? I think the llamas want you to check that."

What was going on? Claire stepped up to the fence and two of the llamas greeted her with a stare that appeared a little more intense, or was that just her imagination? Then she noticed a box—a very small box, perched on the fencepost close to one of the llamas. Was this some kind of joke Dexter was playing?

She reached a shaky hand out to lift the tiny box from the post, amused that the llamas seemed to be watching her closely. Glancing up at Dexter with questioning eyes, she softly spoke, "What is this?"

Dexter was smiling, his gaze moving between Claire and the box. "I think the llamas want you to open it."

Claire lifted the lid off the box, and inside was a small square of pink satin, showcasing the most beautiful diamond ring Claire had ever seen. Was this an engagement ring? Her hands trembled even more, and her vision blurred with tears. She looked up at Dexter, but he was now going down on one bended knee.

"Even though we haven't known each other very long, I have no doubt that you're the lady for me. I love you and always will. Will you marry me, Claire Durham?"

And with llamas witnessing this special event, Claire said yes, and he stood to kiss her. He slipped the ring on her finger, and they kissed again.

"This is the most wonderful Valentine's surprise ever. I love you, Dexter." The crunch of gravel as Howard's car turned into her driveway caused Claire to turn, and a beaming Marcy was grinning from the passenger seat.

The couple rushed toward Claire and Dexter, laughing. They snapped photos of Claire and Dexter with the llamas in the background. She thought her heart might burst.

"Wait, you knew about this?" Claire frowned at Marcy, then Howard. They both nodded and grinned sheepishly.

"Dexter knew somebody needed to arrive to snap photos, and he didn't want to ask a llama, since he wasn't sure about their skills with a camera." Everyone laughed.

"No worries, because we picked up our food at Retha's Diner, and it's in the car. We'll join you in the kitchen unless you want to be alone," Howard spoke, his arm wrapped around Marcy's shoulders.

Claire and Dexter agreed their best friends should join them for their engagement meal, so minutes later the four adults sat at the kitchen table, eating and laughing together.

As Howard teased his buddy about plans to become a married man, Dexter grinned and reached for Claire's hand. "How could I not love this lady? She's not only helped me realize I could love country living, but she's even convinced me that llamas are lovable critters. Who would've thought Dexter Jennings would develop a fondness for llamas?"

They laughed, and Claire had never been happier in her life. She lifted her glass of sweet iced tea and grinned. "To laughter, love, and llamas." Her friends agreed, but especially her fiancé.

~ ~ ~

Epilogue

One Year Later

Claire and Dexter invited Marcy and Howard for a Valentine's Day dinner, complete with red velvet cake for dessert. When their friends arrived, hugs and laughter abounded. Marcy exclaimed over all the special Valentine decorations placed throughout the farmhouse.

Howard had recently given Marcy an engagement ring, and they were planning a June wedding. "I hope you don't mind that I'm copying you, but your June wedding this past year was gorgeous." Marcy beamed at Claire.

"Of course not. I'm thrilled for you and Howard, and June is a great month for a wedding." The women chattered about wedding plans while Dexter updated Howard on the small realty company he now worked for in Peach Grove.

A few minutes before the meal was on the table, Marcy giggled and announced that she'd had a special gift made for Claire. "This is in honor of the fact that your neighbor sold his llamas to you, so now they're officially yours."

Claire peeked into the gift bag and lifted out a soft pink shirt, bearing the words, LLAMA MAMA. She squealed and hugged Marcy. "I love this! And it's perfect, since I have become a doting caregiver for the critters. Thankfully, my cats aren't jealous, though, since the llamas don't come inside the house."

"At least, not yet." Dexter added, as everyone laughed heartily.

Claire thanked Marcy again and told everyone to take their seats, and she'd set the spaghetti, salad, and bread on the table so they could eat. "Dexter is going to offer a blessing for our food." She was so thankful her husband had renewed his relationship with the Lord shortly before their wedding. Dexter had even become active helping at the Peach Grove church.

After Dexter gave a heartfelt blessing, Claire smiled at her friends. "I love my shirt, Marcy."

Marcy appeared pleased and commented that she thought Llama Mama was a perfect name for Claire.

Dexter cleared his throat, gave his wife an adoring look, and put his arm around her. "Well, Claire won't only be a llama mama, but she'll be a human mama in about six months." He placed a kiss on Claire's cheek.

A wide-eyed Marcy squealed, and Howard offered hearty congratulations.

"That's right. Our little one should arrive in August, and we couldn't be happier. And in case you're wondering, the answer is yes. I will be decorating the nursery in a llama theme." As her husband and friends laughed, Claire knew the Lord had blessed her beyond measure. She'd only needed to trust, and He showed her the way. Llamas and all.

THE END

Author Patti Jo Moore is a lifelong Georgia girl who loves Jesus, her family, cats, and coffee. She's a retired kindergarten teacher who now writes "Sweet, Southern Stories" full-time, and loves every minute of it! When she's not writing or spending time with family (including two precious grandgirls), Patti Jo can be found feeding cats---her six and any strays in her neighborhood. She loves connecting with readers and can be found on Facebook at Author Patti Jo Moore. You can also visit her blog at https://catmomscorner.blogspot.com

Patti Jo has 5 novels and 1 novella, all published by Winged Publications (Forget-Me-Not Romance). You can find her books on Amazon, at Patti Jo Moore.

www.ingramcontent.com/pod-product-compliance
Lightning Source LLC
LaVergne TN
LVHW010317070526
838199LV00065B/5596